# ARREST THE ALIBI

## A CEDAR WOODS MYSTERY

ANNE R. TAN

Author's Note: This is a work of fiction. Names, characters, places, and incidents are a product of the author's imagination. Locales and public names are sometimes used for atmospheric purposes. Any resemblance to actual people, living or dead, or to businesses, companies, events, institutions, or locales is completely coincidental.

*To Enny,*
*my sister from another mother*

# 1

## TOILET QUEEN

"How did Aunt Coco break her hip?" Cradling the cell phone between my ear and shoulder, I unplugged the vacuum cleaner. This had to be another ploy to get me home. As much as I loved my kooky relatives, didn't they know I had my own crisis to deal with? I didn't have time for their theatrics.

Aunt Coco had been known to stretch the truth —she probably got that from watching all those Chinese dramas. For the last few months, Aunt Coco had tried to use one excuse or another to get me to move back to my hometown, but she hadn't outfoxed me yet.

"Cedar, this isn't another trick," Joshua Woods said over the phone. "Aunt Coco tripped over her new corgi. Her neighbor found her on the ground in the front yard."

I winced. A broken hip for someone Aunt Coco's age was no joke. Even after recovery, most senior citizens saw a decline in mobility. "When did she get a new dog? I thought she was allergic to pet dander."

"The corgi showed up on her doorstep a few months ago, and it was love at first sight," Josh said.

There was a hint of amusement in my brother's tone. I didn't know what to make of it. When was the last time I'd spoken to my aunt? At least two months. Had it really been that long?

"Does Aunt Coco need surgery?" I asked.

From the corner of my eye, I saw my employer walking past the master bedroom for the third time. Lisa Hilt didn't quite peek in, but she was giving me the stink eye like I should clean rather than chat on the phone. I turned my back to the doorway. What I didn't see, I didn't have to deal with.

"According to the neighbor, it's already done," Josh said. "The old bird went through it like a pro, and she leaves the hospital in a couple of days."

"Is someone helping her at home?"

"She wants you to do it."

I shook my head even though my brother couldn't see me. "What about the Strike Force?"

My aunt had three boys, and each of them worked for a different branch of the military. My brother and I used to jokingly refer to our cousins as the Strike Force since they were deployed to save the world in places we had never even heard of.

"I can't reach them," Josh said. "You know how it is. It's need to know, and apparently, we don't need to know. They will not even get the message until Aunt Coco is back on her feet."

I sighed. Why did I even ask about my cousins? They were never available when we needed them. "Can we hire someone to look after her?"

"Aunt Coco doesn't want to go into a care facility, and I don't blame her. The closest one with open spots is in the next county. And with my work schedule, I can't drive out there every day to check on her. She will be alone there."

"What about in-home care?" I asked.

"Aunt Coco needs someone at home to take care of her," Josh said. "And she wants you."

"Josh, I can't do it." My stomach churned with guilt. I took a deep breath, and when I spoke, my voice came out in a whisper. "I'm hanging by a thread here."

"I know." Josh cleared his throat as if he was considering his words. "When has Aunt Coco asked us for help? She has always been so independent. We owe her."

Josh was right, as always. Uncle Gabriel was Dad's younger brother, and he took us in after our parents' car accident. But it was his wife, Aunt Coco, who gave us a home.

"You have to step up to the plate, Cedar Bear," Josh said. "Aunt Coco would want her girl. I can help, but I still have to work. And it's not exactly like you have a real job."

I sighed. That was the thing about a brother. He was always brutally honest. We were only a year apart and had grown up like twins after his parents adopted me, but every once in a while, he had to remind me of the pecking order in the family. "I have a job, too." I didn't like the defensive tone in my voice.

"Cleaning your hoity-toity friend's McMansion isn't a job." Josh took a deep breath as if calming himself. "Your ex-husband deserves to be shot for the way he treats you."

I stiffened. It wasn't as if I hadn't tried to find a different job, but no one wanted a middle-aged woman who had been out of the job market for two decades. Even my friends had stopped socializing with me like they were afraid a divorce was contagious.

"Once the accountant finishes the financial audit, he will have to pay me alimony," I said. "House cleaning is a stop gap measure until I get my share of the money."

My divorce was final two months ago, but my lawyer had insisted on an audit of my ex-husband's finances because he'd claimed there was no money for spousal support payments. What if something went sideways because I wasn't in San Jose to bird dog this whole mess?

"And my friends came through for me," I said. "They are so embarrassed by the cleaning arrangement, they overpay me. Who else could get thirty dollars an hour to scrub toilets? I'm like the toilet queen."

"Cedar, come home," Josh whispered. "We need you here."

"Are you sure Aunt Coco isn't faking it?" I asked again. What if Aunt Coco had kept my brother in the dark?

Since Aunt Coco and Josh had heard about my ex-husband's side dish—a woman old enough to be his mother—they had worried that I couldn't make it on my own. But I had resisted the temptation of letting my family wrap me up with their love. I would suffocate from all that attention. They often overcompensated for my bio mom's abandonment by giving me the moon. But my pride just couldn't take it.

"I'm at a conference for the rest of this week," Josh said. "I got all this information second hand from Babcia. Aunt Coco probably hasn't recovered enough from her surgery to use her cell phone."

When I had visited, I exchanged greetings with Aunt Coco's neighbor, Babcia, a few times. She probably wouldn't go along with a harebrained scheme for Aunt Coco to fake an injury to get me home.

Josh was silent for a long moment. "Cedar, we need you here. And you need to be here."

I hung up and stared around the meticulously decorated master bedroom. The walls were painted blue with framed paintings of a beach at sunset above the king-sized bed. I had to wear booties over my shoes to keep the plush white carpet clean. I used to have a room like this—sans the white carpet. What an asinine choice.

Now my one-bedroom furnished apartment above the Vietnamese noodle soup restaurant with its yellow linoleum held down at the corners with duct tape was a constant reminder of how far I had fallen from grace. Even at seven in the morning with all the windows wide open, the apartment smelled of beef noodle soup. The food was delicious, but like anything that was always readily available, it was no longer special. And the constant sounds of the family working together and supporting each other below only made me feel even lonelier.

Darn the prenup I had signed in my twenties. Why was I so young and dumb? I had even insisted my ex-husband drive the new car because I didn't feel like I'd deserved it. Who knew twenty years could change a person's perspective about money?

A few minutes later, I found Lisa Hilt lounging next to the pool, flipping through a magazine with a glass of iced tea on the side table next to her. With earbuds in, she didn't hear me approach until I rapped on the side table to get her attention.

Lisa looked every bit the ditzy trophy wife, wearing a short skirt and tight tube top that would pop a blood vessel if she moved a muscle. Hopefully, in another ten years, she would be in a better situation than me. Or maybe not. From my experience, a trophy wife had an even shorter lifespan than a Hollywood actress.

While I had never been a trophy wife, I'd pretended to be one because that was what my ex-husband wanted. Once his tech company took off, he wanted to be just like all the other tech tycoons with their young housewives. And I was willing to do anything so he wouldn't have an excuse to trade me in. Not because I couldn't live without him, but because I finally had a home of my own—a place for me.

Looking up from behind her sunglasses, the fashion magazine forgotten on her lap, Lisa said, "What is it?"

I squinted at the glare from the glistening glass tiles and turquoise water. The stone waterfall burbled and tumbled, drowning out the constant traffic noise in the background. Even a multimillion-dollar home in the Bay Area had to deal with the urban sounds of people living right next to and on top of each other. Wealth was relative, especially when it couldn't even give you elbow room from your neighbors.

"I need some time off to take care of my aunt. She fell and broke her hip," I said.

"How much time do you need?" Lisa asked.

"Initially, a few days," I said, hating the pleading tone that crept into my voice. "I need to get to Mirror Falls first to assess the situation. Maybe I can find someone to provide in-home care for my aunt."

"Who's going to clean my house while you're gone?" Lisa asked.

I shrugged, not quite sure what to say. Swallowing my mounting resentment, I said, "Who cleaned your house before me?"

For a two-person household, Lisa didn't need someone coming in twice a week. She only wanted me here because she could finally feel one up on me. After all, she was still married to her husband, while I was reduced to scrubbing her toilets.

"I fired her so I could give you this job," Lisa said, her tone filled with frost.

My expression didn't change, but I had heard rumors about the former maid and her husband. "I'm sorry about the inconvenience, Lisa. You're a great fr...friend"—I stumbled over the last word but managed to spit it out—"but my aunt is a little old lady. She needs my help. I will come back as soon as I can."

"There's no need to come back." Lisa picked up her cell phone and tapped on the screen. "I've just sent over the funds for today's work. You can pack up your stuff and leave."

I blinked, not sure how to react. I had secretly hoped Lisa would get someone to fill in and hold the job for me. She probably realized I would never return to reign over her social circle again. And now it was time to show me the door.

I swallowed the lump in my throat and hoped that my voice sounded normal. "Thank you for all that you have done for me, Lisa. I am grateful to have a friend like you."

And I was. I still remembered that awful day when I couldn't pay for groceries because my ex-husband had canceled all the joint credit cards, and there was no money left in the checking account. By the time I got home that evening, all the locks were changed.

And Lisa was the only one who gave me a spare bedroom until I got back on my feet. Yes, it mostly fed her pride, but she could have closed the door in my face. Even my brother couldn't wire money over fast enough to help me that night when my world fell apart. Things had become weird between Lisa and me for the last few months as I transitioned from friend to employee. But she had been here for me at the beginning of the end of my marriage.

"Good-bye, Lisa," I said.

"Are you really leaving?" Lisa asked, sitting up on the lounge chair. The magazine slid off her lap and onto the ground.

"I need to take care of my aunt," I said, heading

toward the house. What did Lisa expect? That I would grovel for the time off?

"Wait! Who's going to do my cleaning?" Lisa called after me.

I didn't answer and continued into the house. As I lugged the vacuum cleaner back into the closet in the hall, I held my head up high and prayed that I wouldn't start crying until I was back in my truck. I had tried to hold on to the life I'd known by my fingertips, but it looked like that life was finally done with me.

## 2

## STIFF COMPETITION

The next morning, at the crack of dawn, I packed my meager possessions into the ten-year-old pickup truck—the only thing I got from the divorce—for the drive north to Trinity County. I left the door key in the mail slot for my apartment unit.

I had called my landlord and given notice yesterday, and he was more than happy to have me move out. He had family coming over from Vietnam who needed housing. If I was looking for another sign this phase of my life was over, this was it.

I ignored the tightness in my chest, focusing on the curvy mountain road. The Woods family had adopted me from a Chinese orphanage when I was a one-year-old. Even with all the tragedies in my life, I had known nothing but love from my adopted family.

I got to town by nine in the morning and made my way slowly through the historic Old Town area. In the twenty years that I had lived in the Bay Area, my hometown had acquired two additional stoplights—for a total of four stoplights—and a gazillion signs advertising recreational activities around Trinity Lake.

In Old Town, the buildings mostly had board and batten siding with false fronts with the occasional cottage or craftsman house thrown in to break up the monotony. The Queen Anne mansion that used to belong to the richest family in the county was now a bed-and-breakfast inn, and the huge yard converted into a community park. In the town square was an ancient watermill that now doubled as a visitor center.

Gone were the general and hardware stores of my youth. The shops were an assortment of antique shops and gift shops selling knickknacks, souvenirs, and handmade soaps and lotions from locally grown herbs. They had even built a boardwalk, which doubled as the sidewalk, with wood benches for seating along Main Street to give it a more old-time vibe. When did Mirror Falls become a tourist town?

And even stranger, when did the townsfolk pay for fancy coffee and tea? Mirror Falls was a mountain town where the residents still hunted for their meat and made fun of city yuppies who liked their frou-frou coffee. Or at least they did when I'd left town.

According to my brother, Aunt Coco sunk the rest of her retirement money into a tea shop. At her age! Who gave her the ridiculous idea she needed the stress of running a small business?

If I counted the cafe in the organic co-op supermarket—I couldn't believe there was one in town— there were a total of three coffee shops. And one of them, Fiona's Fine Coffees and Teas, was probably the tea shop's biggest competitor. Even the ice cream parlor sold iced teas. How was Aunt Coco's tea shop supposed to compete with the established businesses? Maybe she could convert it to a tea room, but that was even riskier and more expensive, and none of us had any restaurant experience. Geez, what a mess.

Following my older brother's directions in his text message, I pulled up next to a rundown building on the edge of Main Street. The false-front building had been vacant for years and reportedly haunted, which was how my aunt could afford the purchase.

According to Josh, every previous business at this location had closed within the first year. If I were superstitious, I would say this place had bad juju.

As I stared over the hood of my pickup truck and at the shop windows, my heart sank. What did I know about remodeling or running a small business? I was a former teacher who had given up my career after marriage to raise a family that never materialized. I didn't consider myself a failure, but I hadn't achieved much either. The most I could say was that I'd survived.

The tea shop was scheduled to open in a month, right before the Old Town Fall Festival. If all the stars aligned, it would bring in a lot of foot traffic and holiday shopping—and my aunt could recoup some of her money.

I took a deep breath, got out of the truck, and checked my brother's text message again. I had gotten here in time for the lumber delivery. With Josh out of town, Aunt Coco in the hospital, and the contractor at another job site, it was up to me to make sure the delivery person didn't dump the lumber at an inconvenient location.

The delivery person should be here within the next ten minutes. Even though I knew no one was inside the tea shop, I tried the door handle anyway.

The door handle turned, and I swung open the door. And this was why someone needed to be here to take care of things. Even though there probably wasn't anything of value, a vandal could make a mess, and it would cost more money for the repairs.

Or did someone break in? My pulse jumped at the thought. Other than the tools the contractor had left behind, there was nothing of value in the tea shop. A faint noise came from the back of the building. I glanced around and grabbed the hammer from the toolbox.

Should I call out? But the intruder might escape through the back door. Or should I try to sneak up on him and take him down? Even as this thought crossed my mind, I felt silly for thinking about it. At five foot two inches and slightly heavier than a wet towel—thanks to all the weight I'd lost from the stress of the divorce—the only thing I could take down might be a squawking chicken.

I bit my lower lip, preparing to call out.

"I don't need to steal your baker," Aunt Coco said. "I've already got someone lined up for the job."

I cocked my ear toward the rear of the shop. What was my aunt doing here? Shouldn't she be at the hospital recovering from her surgery? A sudden thought hit me, and I narrowed my eyes in annoyance. The broken hip was another ploy to get me to come home. My aunt was still a wily old fox, and I had been outmaneuvered.

"My cashier saw you talking to Chrissy Lane," an unfamiliar voice said. The person spoke in a high-pitched tone that grated like fingernails on a chalkboard. She was either excited or very angry.

Aunt Coco laughed. "I only asked where she went for culinary school. It's no crime to make small talk."

I stepped through the front room and went into the kitchen. From there, on the right, was a small room. It probably was an office or storage space. Sure enough, I found Aunt Coco behind her desk, leaning back in her chair, and a woman towered over her on the other side.

The stranger was about my age—in her mid-forties—with a pinched, triangular face. Her gray eyes glared at my aunt, and her hands were curled into fists. She placed both hands on top of the desk and leaned into my aunt's personal space. This power play rubbed me the wrong way. This woman wasn't a happy camper, and she wasn't afraid to use her greater height and strength to intimidate an elderly person.

"Stay away from my staff," the woman said through gritted teeth.

Aunt Coco straightened to her full five feet. "If you'd do right by your staff, you wouldn't have to worry about them jumping ship."

The woman's face grew even redder, and a vein started to throb on the side of her forehead. At the rate things were going, the woman might have a heart attack or a stroke. Time to break the tension.

I knocked on the doorframe. "Surprise, surprise. I'm back."

The two women swiveled their heads to stare at me. Aunt Coco blinked, and a guilty expression crossed her face. I gave her a slight shake of my head. She was so busted.

The other woman straightened, removing her hands from the desk. She visibly smoothed out the angry lines on her forehead and regarded me with fake calm. The throbbing vein on the side of her head gave away her true feelings. Maybe she was afraid there would be a witness.

"Aunt Coco, I thought you were in the hospital," I said. While I would forgive my aunt for anything, it didn't mean I would let it slide. This was as good a time as any to throw a small fit.

People usually didn't want to stick around for

family arguments. And now that there were the two of us, maybe this would shift the power in the room, and the angry woman would leave before we needed to call the cops.

I could see the woman studying me from the corner of my eye. Her gaze swiveled back and forth between me and Aunt Coco. Her eyes no longer flashed with anger, but there was a guarded expression on her face. Yep, she was definitely afraid of having a witness.

Hurling one final scowl at my aunt, the woman spun on her heels and stalked out of the room. I took a step back to avoid getting shoved out of the way. My aunt opened her mouth, and I placed a finger to my lips, hushing her. I glanced over my shoulder and listened. I didn't know what was going on here, but I wasn't letting my guard down yet. The angry woman might sneak up behind me or listen in on our conversation.

The front door slammed shut, rattling the office door. I exhaled, and the tension left my shoulders. My forearm ached, and I glanced down to see that I was clutching the hammer in my gloved hand. Oh no. Maybe this was why the woman had backed down.

Aunt Coco jumped out of her chair and wrapped

me in a warm hug. Her hand removed the hammer, and she set it down on her desk.

I crossed my arms and gave my aunt a deadpan expression. "Did you think I was going to use it on you?"

"No, but it never hurts to close that window of possibility," Aunt Coco said, giving me a sheepish grin. She spread her arms out again. "Cedar Bear, welcome home, baby girl."

And the next thing I knew, I was wrapped up in another tight hug. My aunt's silver hair tickled my nose. I pulled away from the hug.

Blinking back the tears in my eyes, I stepped back to put distance between us. I was supposed to be upset at my aunt's big fat lie. She wasn't duping me with her over-the-top motherly act, though I knew deep down it wasn't completely an act. I was the apple of my aunt's eye—standing above the shoulders of her sons.

I checked out my aunt from head to toe. I hadn't seen much of her in the last year, wrapped up as I was in my personal crisis.

For as long as I could remember, my aunt had been round and squishy, like a gigantic body pillow. Even her face and upside-down bowl haircut was round, though in recent years she had acquired the little old lady perm for her thinning hair. She used to have cat-eye framed glasses, but her cataract surgery a few years ago gave her perfect sight, which I was jealous of since everything was a blur without my contacts or glasses. My greatest fear was being stranded somewhere without my glasses.

"You are looking mighty perky for someone who supposedly has a broken hip," I said.

Aunt Coco shrugged, her hands up in the air like she had no clue why I would be upset. "I never said I had a broken hip. There must be some kind of miscommunication here."

"Josh said that you said—"

"Cedar Bear, are you sure Josh spoke to me?"

The question was innocent enough, but I could hear the fine print in it. The technicality that covered the shades of gray. My aunt might have been a lawyer in a previous life.

I reviewed the conversation I had with my brother. She was right. He said her neighbor called him after Aunt Coco fell. It was her neighbor who said my aunt broke her hip and went through surgery. Since Josh was at a conference, he didn't have time to follow up. And her doctor wouldn't have told him anything because of privacy laws.

"Why did your neighbor think you have a broken hip?" I blurted out.

Aunt Coco waved her hand dismissively. "Babcia is hard of hearing—though she would never admit it. She misses half of the conversation and fills in the blanks with whatever pops into her head."

I gaped at my aunt. I'd upended my life because someone liked to fill in the blanks like this was a Mad Libs story. "How come you didn't stop Babcia from calling Josh?"

Aunt Coco stared at me like I was the village idiot. "What makes you think I have any control over Babcia? She knows everyone in town and talks to whoever she wants."

I rubbed my temples. Done was done. One way or the other, I was back in town. "Who was that angry woman? And what is going on between the two of you?"

Before Aunt Coco got a chance to answer my questions, a beeping sound filled the air. She cocked her head, listening intently, and her eyes widened. "The delivery truck!" She brushed past me and hastened to the front door.

My heart sank. Oh no. My whole purpose for waking at the crack of dawn was to get to town to meet the delivery truck. I spun on my heels and darted after my aunt. Something in front of the store clunked and screeched like some kind of air pressure was released.

Outside the shop, on the edge of the boardwalk, Aunt Coco waved a hand at the back of the delivery truck. "You can't just leave the lumber here."

A hand stuck out of the delivery truck, waving back at her. "Sorry, lady. I called the phone number on the invoice, but no one picked up." The truck shifted into gear. "I have to get to my next stop."

"We're not supposed to block the parking spots," Aunt Coco said, gesturing at the pile of lumber laid out across three painted lines on the street.

I heard a shuffling noise from behind me and turned to find the angry woman from earlier standing in front of a doorway. I glanced at the lettering on the window—Fiona's Fine Coffees and Teas. The angry woman was a business rival.

"I'm calling code enforcement," Fiona said. "And then I am calling the cops. Your niece can't go around threatening law-abiding citizens with a hammer."

Aunt Coco placed both hands on her hips. She was in battle mode. "Now hold up—"

Fiona stormed back into the coffee shop and

slammed the door shut, ending the conversation like a petulant child.

I groaned inwardly. Maybe code enforcement and the cops were reasonable people. What if I got detained for my role in what looked to be a long-standing feud?

## 3

## EVIL BUN

I stared at the pile of lumber on the street. Aunt Coco and I might be fairly healthy for our age, but neither one of us was strong enough to drag all the pieces inside the tea shop.

Aunt Coco spoke into her smartwatch. "Hey smarty-pants, call Skywalker."

I blinked. What was my aunt doing? Had she really gone senile? Or was this a nickname for someone on her contacts list?

As the ex-wife of a tech tycoon, I had a love-hate relationship with technology. Previously, I had spent my days pretending to be a budding novelist and planning parties and charity events. The only thing I needed was my cell phone and an internet signal for my laptop. My aunt, however, had always been up to speed on the latest technology. It probably had to do with Uncle Gabriel and the Strike Force's top-secret government work.

Aunt Coco finished her call, and I missed all of it while I gathered wool.

A vehicle pulled up, and a man got out with a lanyard name badge hanging around his neck. I couldn't make out his name. Even with my contact lenses, I didn't have 20/20 vision. He was in his early thirties, tall, dark, and handsome. These days, most young men were handsome in a nonsexual way. Actually, younger people in general made me miss my youth. I didn't know if this was a byproduct of my divorce. Sometimes I felt like I had fallen asleep and woken up a middle-aged woman. I prayed that I'd snap out of this soon. It was exhausting to live with regrets.

The man opened the compartment in his clipboard and pulled out an official document, probably a citation notice. Code enforcement was here. Oh, joy. I wondered if the cops were also on their way.

"Hi, Duncan," Aunt Coco said, waving at him like they were old friends. "Have you met my niece?" She gestured at me. "Cedar, this is Duncan Spencer."

Duncan tipped his chin at me and glanced at the pile of lumber on the street. "Now look here, Coco.

You know you can't block the parking spots. I suggest you get someone to move this, or I will have to give you a citation." His voice was deep and booming like an announcer at a ballgame with a bad microphone.

"I got someone coming over with a forklift," Aunt Coco said. "We'll put the lumber in the alley behind the shops."

Duncan sighed and glanced at the coffee shop. He gave Aunt Coco a long-suffering look. "I'm tired of coming out here every day since you bought this place. Next time, you'll definitely get a citation. Someone has to pay for my time."

Aunt Coco bristled. "Then you should give a citation to your aunt for all these false alarms."

My eyes widened. "Wait a minute. You're related to Fiona? Isn't this like nepotism or a conflict of interest?"

Duncan glanced at the overcast gray sky and sighed. He ignored my questions, probably because he knew there was a conflict of interest with his aunt asking him to harass her new business rival. "Coco, you and my aunt need to figure this out. This feud between the two of you is getting ridiculous. Even Everly was complaining about it."

A police cruiser pulled up behind the code

enforcement vehicle. A uniformed officer got out, and from the body shape, I could tell this person was a woman. I didn't bother squinting at the name badge. It would take a miracle for me to make out the letters.

"Speak of the devil." Duncan tucked the clipboard underneath an arm and stepped back like he was getting ready to watch a show. He didn't even need a bowl of popcorn to make it obvious.

The officer stomped over with a scowl that twisted her heart-shaped face. She was about my age, but powerfully built. She probably trained daily like an athlete. Her uniform was crisp, clean and pressed, and the badge clipped to her belt glinted in the sunlight. Her dark brown hair was showing signs of gray at the temples and pulled back in a no-nonsense bun.

"Hi, Everly," Aunt Coco said, smiling serenely like this was a routine visit. Maybe it was. "Do you remember Cedar?" She gestured at me. "The two of you were in elementary school together."

"It's Chief Blunt, ma'am," the woman said.

I didn't remember having a friend called Everly Blunt. The only person I knew who came close was Evil Bun, but she was the school bully. What was the bully's real name? I squinted at the police chief.

Who cared? It was a long time ago. And I didn't believe Evil Bun had what it took to become a cop anyway. That girl was trouble and got suspended more times than I had fingers. She probably continued to travel down the wrong side of the law and stayed there.

Chief Blunt turned to look me in the eye, and I shifted my gaze to the faint line of a long-ago scar on her chin. Shifting my gaze probably made me look guilty, but cop eyes always felt like they could see into my soul. I peeked up, and the chief was still staring at me, unblinking. This was getting creepy.

I studied her chin, and something tingled in the back of my mind. That scar looked mighty familiar. I had seen it before. And it hit me. The scar was a keepsake from my charging head butt. My heart sank, and my grip on the column loosened. I tumbled off the boardwalk and fell onto the road. Luckily, it was only a twelve-inch drop. I stumbled and bumped into Duncan.

Oh no. Maybe Evil Bun didn't remember me. After all, the fight had happened more than thirty-five years ago.

Duncan grabbed my arm and hauled me up. For a skinny guy, he had a lot of strength. "Are you okay?"

I nodded. "Just feeling a little lightheaded." Which was true. I didn't think Evil Bun would frame me for anything, but she might detain me for amusement. I jerked my thumb towards the tea shop. "I should probably go inside and sit down for a bit." And hopefully, Evil Bun would be gone by the time I "felt better."

"I'll come with," Chief Blunt said. "I have some questions for you, Weird Wood."

My answering smile wobbled. I didn't know why I expected to blend into the background. In my childhood, folks in town adopted children from the same county. Whereas, I was the Chinese orphan from China, and I stuck out no matter how much I twisted myself into a pretzel to fit in. I cocked a hip and planted a hand on it. "It's Cedar Woods. Come on. You're a professional now, so act like one."

As soon as the words left my mouth, I wanted to kick myself. Aunt Coco's grin grew even wider. Duncan's jaw dropped, just like the kids in the playground did on that fateful day when I'd dared to stand up to the school bully. Sure, I had gotten beat up, but I didn't make it easy for Evil Bun.

Chief Blunt gave me a tight-lipped smile. "Sorry, ma'am. That slipped out." She rubbed the side of her chin where the scar was located.

The hair on the back of my neck stiffened. A fake polite Evil Bun meant she had learned to hide her evil ways. If I were to stay in town, there would be payback. Luckily, I wasn't staying.

Chief Blunt continued to stare at me. "Duncan, can you get your aunt? I need to take her statement." She rested her hand next to the holster on her hip, the fingers brushing the handle of her gun.

I shivered at the gesture. If this wasn't a threat, I didn't know what was.

"It's a good thing we're out in the middle of the street," Aunt Coco said, crossing her arms. "If you plan to shoot us, I'm glad there will be witnesses."

"The generosity of the annual budget gets me one box of bullets," Chief Blunt said. "And you two are not bullet worthy." She pulled out a notebook and flipped to a blank page. "Let's hear your side of the story, Cedar. Why are you threatening Fiona with a hammer?"

I explained what had happened. "It's a misunderstanding."

Chief Blunt scribbled on her notepad. "So your aunt was having a yelling match with Fiona?" she read from her notes.

From what I had gathered so far, this sounded like a regular occurrence between my aunt and the coffee shop owner. Why was Evil Bun making it sound like I had the motivation to threaten Fiona? Was she trying to invent a reason to haul me into jail? That would be so unethical...so evil.

"Voices were raised, but I wouldn't call this a yelling match," I said, glancing at my aunt.

Aunt Coco came over and stood next to me, so now we were both flanking Chief Blunt. With both hands on her hips, my aunt said, "There was no yelling match. Fiona is looking for any excuse to make trouble for me. You've been called out here for one thing or another several times a week. I don't know about you, but I am tired of this harassment. Can this be considered a hate crime?"

Chief Blunt paused, her pen poised over her notebook. "What do you mean?"

"I'm Chinese," Aunt Coco said.

"Are you playing the race card?" Chief Blunt said.

"Will it work?" Aunt Coco said.

Chief Blunt rubbed her temple. "Since Fiona also harasses the other coffee shop owners in town, I don't think she's targeting you because you're Chinese. This is an equal opportunity harassment."

"Oh." Aunt Coco looked crestfallen. "I was hoping to get to play the sympathy card in my next Survivors Club meeting."

The Survivors Club was my aunt's book club. The ladies discussed self-help books to help them overcome their grief. Apparently, it worked better than therapy.

Chief Blunt glanced at me, then at my aunt, and back to me again as if to say it was my responsibility to control my aunt.

I blinked back at Evil Bun and gave her a blank expression. Fat chance I would rein in my aunt. If I had to deal with my aunt's circular logic, then everyone should have their share of the frustration too.

Someone screamed, and something crashed to the ground. The noise came from the coffee shop. Chief Blunt drew her gun, leaped up on the boardwalk, and dashed inside the shop.

I gaped in shock at the police chief's rapid movements, and the shop door slamming shut behind her. The last time I had moved that fast was when I was in high school. Mental note to self—do not get into any kind of physical altercation with Evil Bun. She was definitely out of my weight class.

Aunt Coco was already at the coffee shop door when I finally stopped gathering wool. "Are you coming, girl, or are you planning to catch flies with your open mouth?"

I joined my aunt, and the two of us stepped inside. The coffee shop had wood-paneled walls and dim lighting with a bar up against one wall, giving it an old-fashioned saloon vibe, which felt strange for a coffee shop.

The scent of burned coffee—the scent you would find in the middle of the night at a diner off the highway—was overpowering. Fine coffee was more of a hope and prayer in this establishment. There were a number of tables and chairs, but the shop was empty. No customers. No wonder Fiona was afraid of competition.

We stepped through the double saloon doors to the kitchen. Both Chief Blunt and Duncan had their backs to us.

"Everything okay?" Aunt Coco called out.

My gaze dropped to the floor, and I gasped in horror, covering my mouth with my hands. Fiona was stretched out on the floor, her eyes closed. If it weren't for the puddle of blood, I would think she was sleeping. Next to her motionless body was a bloody hammer.

## 4

## ALL HAMMERS LOOK THE SAME

I gripped the doorframe to anchor myself. I felt as if I were floating above the scene, watching it from a great distance. Someone spoke, but I couldn't make out the words. I heard only the rushing noise in my ears. My vision became white around the edges, and I could only see the body and the blood. I would not pass out. I would not pass out.

Movement from the corner of my eye caught my attention. Aunt Coco's silver hair. Oh no. My elderly aunt shouldn't look at this scene. What if she had a heart attack from the shock? It took all of my strength to drag my gaze away from the bloody hammer.

I felt a snap like I came back inside my body. I

37

swiveled my head and found Aunt Coco inches from Fiona, hunched over the body like she was on the forensic team. Luckily, she had the sense to not touch anything.

"Aunt Coco, get back here," I whispered. For some reason, it felt wrong to speak normally around a dead body. "What are you doing?"

Chief Blunt jerked up from staring at the body. Her face was ashen. She still gripped her gun like she was expecting a shoot-out. For a second, I felt bad for her. How many murders had she investigated in Mirror Falls? Her job probably consisted of directing traffic during the tourist season, arresting drunks, and busting up wild parties. She blinked and put the gun back into her holster.

"Everybody, back onto the street," Chief Blunt said. Her voice came out gruffer than usual. "Do not touch anything."

All of us stumbled outside. Duncan, with a dazed expression on his face, collapsed onto the wooden bench on the boardwalk.

Aunt Coco pulled me aside and whispered, "How did the hammer get inside the coffee shop?"

It took me a second to register what my aunt was asking. "That can't be our hammer. We were both on the street the entire time. We have witnesses. Even the most incompetent police work couldn't have us at two places at the same time."

Aunt Coco chewed her lower lip. "It sure looked like the hammer from the tea shop."

"All hammers look the same," I said in full denial mode. This was like a car accident where the first person to admit fault was automatically the guilty one. I shook my head. "No, this had nothing to do with us."

Aunt Coco grabbed my hand and tugged me toward the tea shop. "I have an uneasy feeling about this. Let's go check."

My aunt's hand was clammy. She might look fine on the outside, but she was shaken up. And she seemed genuinely concerned about the hammer. Now I was worried as well.

There was the sound of an approaching vehicle, and someone called out, "Hey, Coco. Is this the lumber?"

Aunt Coco glanced at the person and waved. "Luke, dear, come here."

So, this was the Skywalker in my aunt's contacts list. He was about my age and tall, with a lanky frame that suggested he was used to physical activity.

His dark black hair was gray at the temples and short but still had enough length to be tussled by the wind. He definitely would be my pick for a blind date.

Luke got out of the car, and I kid you not, he had on a stereotypical lumberjack outfit—red and black plaid shirt and dark blue jeans with work boots, except he was Asian, probably Korean or Japanese. He climbed the steps to the boardwalk. His brown eyes met my gaze and then he ignored me. He addressed my aunt, "What is it?"

"Is your last name Skywalker?" I asked, stepping in front of him so he couldn't ignore me.

"That's a joke between me and your aunt," Luke said, not bothering to make eye contact.

I raised an eyebrow. He knew who I was, which meant my aunt had been talking about me to him. I wonder what else my aunt might have told him. Hopefully, she didn't say anything about my marital status. I wasn't embarrassed, but the divorce was still so recent that I couldn't handle any sympathy or anger about the situation.

I held out my hand. "I am Cedar Woods."

Luke stared at my hand for a long moment as if debating whether or not he could ignore it.

I wasn't sure why, but I bristled at the look of distaste on his face. Was he a germophobe? Or just socially awkward? Or maybe I was embarrassed by my initial attraction and his obvious rejection of it. I couldn't explain why, but I wanted Luke to acknowledge me.

"Sora Kai, but I go by my middle name," Luke said.

So, he was Japanese. His name literally translated to the sky and the sea. I knew those three years of Japanese in high school would amount to something. By this time my hand had been dangling between us for far too long for me to withdraw without obvious embarrassment.

Luke glanced at my aunt. "You want me to move the lumber to the back alley?"

"Something important came up," Aunt Coco said. "We need to find a hammer." She disappeared inside the tea shop.

With that, Luke strode after my aunt. I dropped my hand and followed the two of them. I wasn't sure how I had offended Luke, but I was irritated with the man. I set the thought aside. There was time to noodle on this later.

I was equally curious to see if our hammer was the murder weapon. The front door of the tea shop was visible the entire time we were out on the street, and I didn't see anyone near it.

At the doorway to the office, Aunt Coco cried out, "The hammer. It's gone."

I joined my aunt to stare at the empty spot on her desk. A sense of dread settled in the pit of my stomach. I shook my head in disbelief. Did someone set me up as Fiona's murderer?

Up until this morning, I didn't even know the woman. But since Fiona had been busy telling everyone I had threatened her with a hammer, this would make me the prime suspect. Except, I had worn gloves, and the only fingerprints on the hammer belonged to my aunt.

Maybe someone was trying to set up my aunt? But how did this person know my aunt's fingerprints would be on the hammer?

No, this setup wasn't a personal attack on me or my aunt. It was an opportunity the murderer had taken advantage of to throw the cops off the real trail. Yes, this made more sense.

Luke glanced at the desk and then back at the two of us. "I got a hammer in the back of my truck."

Aunt Coco's eyes flicked from side to side as if looking for an explanation. "Someone must have come in from the back door." She moved as if she was going to check, and I grabbed her arm to stop her.

"We don't want to touch anything," I said. "This could be a crime scene. Let's go back out front and wait for the forensic team."

"What forensic team?" Aunt Coco said. "Your brother's the county coroner, and he's at the conference. Everly will have to ask the feds for help. That might take days, if not weeks."

I blinked, not quite sure what to think. I knew a small town had limited resources, but didn't they have people to process a crime scene? No wonder crimes became cold cases and innocent people were railroaded for crimes they didn't commit.

I pressed a hand to the fluttering in my stomach. What if Evil Bun wanted to throw me in jail? Was she related to Fiona? Maybe there would be a conflict of interest, and Evil Bun would have to step aside from this investigation.

It didn't matter. I was still a suspect. They would say I killed Fiona to aid my aunt. Or they might say my aunt and I were in it together. One or both of us would be going to jail.

Luke studied my aunt with a worried gaze. "What's going on here? How can I help?"

I gave Luke a sideways glance. Sure, there was a

thing called small-town hospitality, but he was a stranger to me. But then again, I didn't know the nature of his relationship with my aunt. For all I knew, they might regard each other like family.

Aunt Coco quickly summarized what had happened next door.

Luke's brown eyes widened in disbelief. "I knew it, Coco. You're going to jail." He ran a hand through his black hair. "How am I going to explain this to Josh? He's going to kill me."

"What does my brother have to do with it?" I said.

Luke ignored my question, and I wanted to stomp my feet in frustration. Why wasn't someone filling me in? Who was Luke, and how was he associated with my brother?

Wait a minute. Was Luke in a relationship with my brother? Was this why my brother never got married? I couldn't believe that I'd never suspected this.

"It wasn't my fault," Aunt Coco said, dragging me from my thoughts.

One glance at my aunt's taut face was enough for me to refocus on our current situation. The most important thing at the moment was to make sure we weren't hauled off to jail.

"I didn't antagonize Fiona on purpose," Aunt Coco said. "She came over this morning shouting about how the construction in the tea shop was driving away her customers. My contractor isn't even working today."

"So there was no reason for her to complain?" Luke said.

Aunt Coco nodded. "And what customers? Who would want to drink that nasty coffee? And with that prickly personality, I wouldn't be surprised if Fiona had enemies up the wazoo."

My aunt had gotten over her shock and was now in full rant mode. She did that from time to time, to let off a little steam. All of us were amused by her tirades, and life went on as usual once she got it out of her system.

However, the fact that Aunt Coco had recovered so quickly also got me worried. What if Evil Bun used this as a sign that my aunt had something to do with Fiona's death?

*Bang! Bang!*

The three of us jumped at the sudden racket. Someone was pounding on a metal door.

"Someone is at the back door," Aunt Coco said. She hurried out of the office.

I was hot on her heels. As my aunt reached to

push the metal bar to unlatch the door, I blocked the move.

"Wait!" I said. "What if there are fingerprints from the hammer thief?" Using my elbow, I pushed open the back door.

Chief Blunt was on the other side, glaring at us. "Looks like I got my killer."

I ignored her comment and opened the door wide, holding it in place with the kick stop. I stepped into the alley behind the shops, and Evil Bun had to back up or I would have stepped on her toes. Now that we were standing side-by-side, she towered over me in her work boots by a good five inches, which made her about five foot nine. Oh, joy.

Luke and Aunt Coco followed me outside. The back alley was wide enough for a small delivery truck to get through. Wood fencing ran the length of the alley, marking the side yards for the homes on the other side. A dumpster located in the middle of the alley serviced all the shops on this block. There was nothing remarkable about the alley, and nothing to point to my aunt's shop as the home of the murderer. Evil Bun was probably blowing smoke, hoping we would crumble with fear.

Luke folded his arms. "I wouldn't make any accusation until you're done processing the crime scene.

Josh is at a conference this week. Who is collecting the body?"

Aunt Coco looked as if she was about to argue, but promptly closed her mouth. Smart woman. As a modern, independent woman, I didn't need a man to fight for me. However, sometimes it helped to have one throw his weight around. It moved the focus of attention away from me, and I could do my thing in the wings.

I shifted to peer at the front side of the door. There! A bloody spot on the handle. I couldn't make out a fingerprint, and that was probably the intent. Its job wasn't to help find the murderer, but to point the finger at us—in case the hammer didn't do the trick. That low down dirty dog.

"I need the three of you to sit on the bench in front," Chief Blunt said. "If you leave before I say you can, I am getting a warrant for your arrest."

The three of us traipsed back through the tea shop as instructed and sat next to Duncan on the wooden benches like naughty children. I glanced at the display screen on my cell phone. It was already noon, and foot traffic was picking up. All the town folk greeted my aunt and gawked at the crime scene tape closing off the coffee shop and tea shop. This wasn't the homecoming I had envisioned.

"Kelly isn't gonna like this," Luke muttered to himself.

"Who is Kelly?" I asked, fully expecting him to ignore my question like earlier.

"Your aunt's contractor," Luke said. "He's already nickeled and dimed your aunt for the work. I was out of town and didn't get a chance to look over her contract, or I would have recommended someone else. The guy talks a big game but rarely delivers."

These were more words than Luke had said to me previously combined. Maybe he was warming up to me.

"I'm sure we can resume work on the tea shop in another day or two, when the police finish processing the crime scene," I said. "This shouldn't put us too far behind schedule." I didn't know much about construction, but I did know that time was money.

"Have you forgotten about the comment about borrowing resources from other jurisdictions? Your aunt will probably lose her deposit and her contractor."

"I won't let that happen," I said. "This money is Aunt Coco's retirement."

"I don't see what you can do about it," Luke said.

This time I ignored his comment. In a town

where everyone knew everyone's business, I was sure we could put together a list of suspects. While I preferred to mind my own business, I didn't have a choice here. But if the killer knew I was investigating Fiona's death, I might be next on the hit list.

## 5

## A GOOD DOG

For the next two hours, we were left to cool our heels. Luckily, Luke had convinced the police chief to let him get sandwiches for everyone. And he was smart enough to get one for Chief Blunt before she questioned us individually.

We gave our statements in the front room of the bookshop. Duncan went first, then my aunt, and followed by me. Evil Bun tried to bait me, but I stuck to the facts as I knew them. She asked a handful of questions in several creative ways, but she got the same answers from me over and over again.

Finally, Chief Blunt closed her notebook in disgust. "Please don't leave town."

We stepped back onto the boardwalk, and Chief

Blunt gestured for Luke to follow her inside to give his statement.

Aunt Coco handed the chief a spare key. "Can you lock up once you're done here? I don't want any Tom, Dick, and Harry traipsing through. The contractor would be mighty angry if his tools disappeared."

Chief Blunt took the key, but she didn't look happy with the responsibility. She closed the shop door on us.

"What's next?" I said.

Aunt Coco looked as baffled as me. "I have a feeling Duncan might pressure Everly to arrest someone, probably me. And since his dad is the mayor, I'm going to jail."

"We need to look for a lawyer," I said.

"I got that part covered," Aunt Coco said. "I have Perry Goodwin on speed dial."

I gave my aunt a sideways glance, disturbed that she needed regular access to a lawyer. Since her husband's death, she had been unpredictable. Aunt Coco had always been big on routines and sched-ules. She had to be—raising three boys on her own while her husband went off to save the world, and then later adding Josh and me to the mix.

I was one of those lucky women who had many mothers in my life—my biological mother who I never knew, my adopted mother who died when I was young, and Aunt Coco who raised me like I was her favorite child.

I didn't know if the change in her personality was a cry for attention or if something else was going on. Could it be Alzheimer's? Was something off on her medication? I knew she took a pill for her blood pressure, but she never had a problem with it before.

"Do we need to stick around and wait for Luke to move the lumber?" I asked.

Aunt Coco glanced at the lumber pile. "With all the excitement, I forgot all about that. I think it's fine to leave it here for now. Duncan is probably too preoccupied to give me a citation."

"What if somebody takes it?" I asked.

Aunt Coco pulled a Sharpie marker from her pocket and wrote "Coco Woods" on the top piece of lumber. "Let's go home. We should talk this through with General. Maybe he'll have some ideas about what we need to do next."

"Who's General?"

"My new corgi. He's my husband's reincarnated spirit."

I blinked, not quite sure I had heard correctly. "Can you repeat that?"

"He's your Uncle Gabriel."

"Who is Uncle Gabriel?"

"My new dog."

"And how do you know this?"

"He told me."

I didn't know how to react. A load of bricks landed on my shoulders. If this wasn't a cry for attention, I didn't know what was. I sighed. I didn't have the bandwidth for this at the moment. I would have to noodle on this later. I glanced at the tea shop windows. "Do we need to wait for Luke?"

"He's a big boy. He can get home by himself."

"I was thinking along the line that three heads were better than two."

"I don't know about that," Aunt Coco said. "Luke can be a bit of a nag. When your brother is out of town, Luke takes his role as my babysitter very seriously."

We hopped into my pickup truck and drove the short distance to Aunt Coco's house. During the drive, we rehashed the facts but didn't come to any new conclusion. I parked on the curb in front of the Second Empire two-story home with a finished attic. A brick chimney reached up to the overcast sky. The house was sea foam green with white trim. The tall and narrow windows were framed in by a cinnamon red color that almost matched the burgundy slate roof. The house looked as if it belonged in *Alice and Wonderland* and was perfect for my aunt.

Uncle Gabriel and Aunt Coco had spent most of their adult lives living on one military base or another. They'd never owned a house of their own, and the grand plan was to buy a fixer-upper and spend the first few years of retirement fixing it up. They had moved back to his hometown, bought a house, and started the remodeling.

Unfortunately, my uncle had passed away during the second year of his retirement, leaving my aunt with a fixer-upper that she couldn't sell in the current housing market. And to make it worse, she spent the other half of the retirement money on a tea shop. What was she thinking?

I rubbed my temples. "Do you have any Tylenol? I'm getting a headache."

Aunt Coco patted my shoulder. "Cedar Bear, I'm sorry. This wasn't the homecoming I had planned for you."

I squeezed my aunt's hand. "Let's get inside the house."

Aunt Coco opened the mahogany front door

with the stained-glass panels. The cold brass handle gleamed like it had recently been polished. While my aunt was a wonderful mother figure, she'd always thought a little dirt improved a person's constitution. The idea probably came from raising kids on military bases around the world that weren't in the best conditions.

"Did you hire a cleaning person?" I said.

"No, a little dirt doesn't bother me," Aunt Coco said.

I glanced at the brass handle again. It was far too clean. "I'm surprised there aren't more fingerprints on the door handle."

Aunt Coco waved dismissively. "Oh, that's Molly's doing. She was the former maid for this house. I guess she gets bored and still cleans the house once in a while."

The arrangement sounded strange to me. I couldn't imagine wanting to continue to clean my former employer's house without payment.

As Aunt Coco swung open the door, the pitter-patter of footsteps approached us. Then a joyful yelp. I had expected a puppy, but the corgi that bounded down the staircase was a full-grown adult. And from his stiff movements, it was a much older dog. My aunt had clipped a tiny crocheted green beret, similar to the one my uncle had worn with pride, on the dog's head.

"This is General, huh?" I said, holding out my hand for the dog to sniff.

General ducked under my hand, so that I petted him on the head. Strange. I thought corgis distrusted strangers and were avid barkers. This dog was greeting me like we were old friends.

"How did you find this sweetheart?" I said.

Aunt Coco handed me a pair of indoor slippers. Most Chinese families didn't wear their outdoor shoes inside the house and had extra slippers at hand for guests. I changed out of my shoes.

"General found me," Aunt Coco said. "He showed up on my back door steps on your uncle's death anniversary." A sad look crossed her face, and my heart ached with her. She glanced at the corgi and the look was replaced with a smile. "I've asked around, but no one claimed him. He's mine now."

My gaze flickered between my aunt and her pet. "Does he talk to anyone else? Or is it just you?"

Aunt Coco scratched General's chin. "Just me. I'm the special one."

"How old is General?"

Aunt Coco tapped on the screen of her phone. "Want tea?" At my nod, she tapped on the screen again. At my quizzical look, she said, "Smart kettle. I can turn it on with the app on my phone. It's from your brother."

This explained everything. As much as I loved Josh, I had to admit that he was a bit of a nerd, and socially awkward. He was always gifting us smart devices that, quite frankly, were more trouble than they were worth. At least for me anyway.

It was an interest Josh had in common with my ex-husband, and why my brother took it so hard when he'd found out about my failed marriage. I had seen the writing on the wall for years, but didn't want to deal with the fallout of disappointing my family. I had buried my head in the sand, keeping busy and doing nothing, hoping my failing marriage would miraculously resolve itself.

"The vet doesn't know how old he is," Aunt Coco said.

I blinked and returned to the foyer in my aunt's house. "Who?"

"General. You asked about his age."

"Sorry. I was gathering wool," I said, following my aunt into the kitchen.

"I'm lucky he's not a puppy because I trained

your uncle once, and I'm not up for training him again," Aunt Coco said. "That man always left his wet towels on the floor, and it took two decades to break him of the habit. He told me to invest in the tea shop. Didn't you, sweetie?" She rubbed the dog's head and gave him air kisses.

And here I thought this couldn't get any worse. I knew the elderly were targets for foreign lotteries or a desperate call from a mythical grandchild needing money. I had warned my aunt against all these scams, but I never thought to warn her against taking financial advice from her talking pet.

General padded beside Aunt Coco, his tongue hanging out. He was so cute. I could see why my aunt wanted to think her husband came back in the form of a corgi.

As I stepped into the kitchen, my jaw dropped. It was a complete disaster. My uncle had started removing the countertops but then fell ill. Someone had come in afterwards to remove the rest, exposing the warped wood and mud layer underneath. How come my aunt didn't hire someone to come finish the job? Several cabinet doors were off and stacked in one corner of the room. The refrigerator looked like the only functioning appliance. There was a hot plate on the countertop.

*Please don't tell me my aunt has been using the hot plate to heat up her food*, I thought to myself.

I winced as the headache came crashing down. A flash of anger rose from my chest. This was what happened when I left it to the boys to take care of my aunt for a year while I dealt with my divorce. My cousins and my brother were intelligent men and did important work in their chosen professions, but they were unreliable when it came to taking care of family.

Aunt Coco pulled a bottle of Tylenol from a drawer and handed it and a glass of water to me. She pulled two mugs from a drawer and said, "Black or green?"

I swallowed two pills with the water. "Do you have any of the lavender cream black tea?"

Aunt Coco turned to prepare the tea. "It's your favorite, so I always keep some at hand."

I took several deep breaths to calm down. It wasn't my aunt's fault her kitchen looked like this. "Didn't my cousins make plans last Christmas to finish up the kitchen when they were all in town?"

"They did, but it's rare for them to be together. They had to catch up with their friends, and then the hardware store was closed for the holidays." Aunt Coco shrugged. "And then it was time for them to get back to their work. And Josh can't do any of this. You know how he is. He can't even use a screwdriver without scraping up his fingers."

I sipped my tea to keep from cursing. The Strike Force were going to hear it from me. My aunt wasn't the only one in the family with a tendency to rant once in a while.

I spent the rest of the day bringing in my stuff and putting it in a bedroom on the second floor. Thank goodness I didn't get a room in the finished attic. This house was far too big for the two of us. Maybe I could talk my aunt into renting out a room or two for some extra income. But who would want to rent a room in a house without a functioning kitchen? Like the tea shop, the house also had to be fixed up before we could get any income from it.

Aunt Coco's Social Security and my teacher's pension weren't going to get us very far. I had cashed out my pension early and with all the penalties, it was tiny. Like the house cleaning jobs, it was supposed to be a stop gap measure for the next year or so. But at the rate my ex-husband was dragging his feet, it could be months before I would see any money from him. It had fed his ego that he could afford to have a housewife in the Bay Area. But why did I stupidly listen to him and quit a paying job for volunteer work?

We had a safety net in that the boys would never let us starve, but my pride didn't like the idea of accepting money from them. And I was sure my aunt wouldn't want the strings that came with the money.

## 6

## FUGITIVES

I was on the edge of consciousness when I felt a presence in my room. I know, I know… I'd lost my mind. But when you spent the last few months dealing with my ex-husband, his mistress who later became his wife, and the lawyers, the feeling of being watched wasn't the least bit surprising. I pulled the comforter down, and there was a white light shining on my face. I was about to kick the intruder on the shins when the familiar voice of my aunt penetrated through my sleepy brain.

Aunt Coco waved her cellphone with the flashlight app on over my face. "Cedar Bear, wake up!"

I pushed the phone aside. If the white light had come from a UFO or a ghostly presence, then at least I would still have my privacy. "Aunt Coco! What are you doing? And turn off that light!"

Aunt Coco's smile widened. "Rise and shine, Cedar Bear. I have already given you a whole day to mope around the house. Time to get up and have a good day."

I pulled the comforter over my head. "Aunt Coco, I'm fine. Just leave me alone."

"No can do, Cedar Bear. We have to put together a suspect list and check it twice," Aunt Coco said in a singsong voice and tugged at the comforter.

I held on to the comforter and wrapped my legs around it. "Stop calling me Cedar Bear. I'm not six anymore."

"You're sure acting like it." Aunt Coco gave one mighty yank and jerked the comforter out of my hands. "Now put on your big girl panties."

The palms of my hands burned. "What did you have for breakfast? Wheaties?"

"I don't eat the breakfast of champions." Aunt Coco flexed her biceps. "But I exercise every day."

I sat up in bed and brushed my black hair off my face. When was the last time I washed my hair? I sniffed at a strand of oily hair and wrinkled my nose. "Can't this wait until a decent hour? What time is it? Nine?"

"Six thirty."

I groaned and flopped back into bed. I curled up into a fetal position and covered my face with my hands. "Why do we need to get up this early? Neither one of us has a job."

"We're going to hit the coffee shops," Aunt Coco said. "All of them. They'll be busy, but we can eavesdrop and see what's going around the rumor mill."

"Later. When they are less busy, and the barista has time to talk to us," I mumbled from behind my hands. "The early bird does not catch the worm in this case."

"Let's go have breakfast with Babcia."

I groaned again. I knew what was happening here. My aunt wanted to show me off like I was her new prized possession. After all, how many retirees had their grown children at their beck and call?

"We'll have plenty of time to sleep when we're both in jail." Aunt Coco clapped her hands. "Now let's go."

I showered, dressed, and went downstairs to the kitchen. Aunt Coco sat at the square table overlooking the backyard. She handed me a mug of tea and a fresh blueberry scone. General padded in and got onto Aunt Coco's lap. He watched me eat with attentive eyes like he was hoping I would offer him a crumb. He was definitely a cutie and clearly a comfort to my aunt.

"It looks like Babcia isn't available until this afternoon," Aunt Coco said. "Let's go back to my idea of visiting the coffee shops. And then we can pick up our costumes."

I bit into the scone. Yum. "Did you make this? It's good."

My aunt wasn't much of a cook. Her talent lay in being able to whip up a filling meal for an army any time of day from her pantry and freezer. The meals might not all be tasty, but they got the job done. So I knew she couldn't have baked such a yummy scone, but it didn't cost me anything to flatter her.

Aunt Coco smirked. "You have more faith in me than I give you credit for. While you were still sleeping, I did my three-mile walk and stopped by the bakery."

General's ears perked up, and he left to go into the foyer.

"Someone's at the front door. General has a sixth sense about these things." Aunt Coco tapped on her cell phone, probably to open up the doorbell camera app. "Oh no. It's Everly, and she looks like she had nails for breakfast."

A piece of the scone got stuck on the back of my

throat, and I coughed. I took a gulp of the hot tea, and it burned all the way down. What was Evil Bun doing here? Was she planning to arrest me, my aunt, or both of us?

*Ding dong! Ding dong! Ding dong!*

General padded back into the dining room. I was surprised he didn't bark at the front door.

"What do we do?" I whispered.

"Maybe if we keep real quiet, she'll go away," Aunt Coco said.

I didn't think this would work. The police weren't a door-to-door salesperson. She could bust down the front door.

General woofed and turned to look at the back door.

Aunt Coco shoved her cell phone into her sweater pocket. "That's a brilliant idea."

"What's the brilliant idea?" I asked.

"General thinks we should sneak out from the backyard. There's a gate on the fence that leads to the alley behind the row of houses."

I gaped at my aunt. What kind of cockamamie idea was this? If we ran, wouldn't this make us fugitives? No, Evil Bun couldn't have gotten a warrant for our arrest so quickly. She was probably here to question us some more or to bring us down to the station.

And it was probably well within our rights to ignore her without having to run away like we were guilty.

*Bang! Bang!*

"Coco, I know you're in there," Chief Blunt shouted. "Open the door. I'm in no mood for games."

Aunt Coco ran into the foyer and came back with our shoes. "Cedar, let's go."

I got up, wrapping my napkin around the scone and stuffing it into my pocket. If I was running away from home like a criminal, at least I would have food with me.

I followed my aunt out the back door, down the stairs, into the backyard, and through a gate that opened into a small alley of garages for the homes on this block. These used to be the carriage houses for the Victorian homes. We were completely hidden from the street in front of the house.

When I had pulled the truck into the garage last night I didn't see my aunt's Hummer. "What happened to your car?" I asked.

"It's in the shop," Aunt Coco said, glancing around. There was no one in the alley. "A pole jumped in front of me."

I sighed. I had forgotten about my aunt's horrible driving. It was part of the reason why Uncle Gabriel decided to purchase a house within walking distance to Old Town, so my aunt wouldn't have to drive when he wasn't around.

We trotted to the opening of the alley and headed for Old Town. As I tried to keep up with my aunt, my heart pounded in my chest. I had always been the good kid. I had followed all the rules and was praised by the adults around me. It took me years of therapy to realize this came from being an adoptee. I was afraid that if I acted up, I would be abandoned again.

Running away from the police was the closest I ever came to breaking the rules. A part of me was secretly thrilled. And this scared me more than anything else.

WE MADE it two blocks before we saw the police cruiser rounding the corner. Luckily, Chief Blunt was watching the traffic in the opposite direction and didn't see us. I grabbed my aunt's hand and tugged her behind a redwood tree in someone's front yard.

Aunt Coco scooped General up into her arms, whispering, "Be quiet, my darling. We don't want to get caught."

The police cruiser drove by. We inched around the tree, keeping it between us and the sheriff. We waited a few more minutes before leaving our hiding place.

"Where are we heading?" I removed the now crushed scone from my pocket and nibbled on it. "If Chief Blunt is heading back to the crime scene, we will run into her if we continue in the same direction."

Aunt Coco shrugged. "I have no idea." She glanced down at General. "What now, sweetie?" She cocked her head, listening.

Silence.

The corgi regarded her with placid eyes.

Aunt Coco harrumphed. "He's not answering, the old geezer."

I continued to eat the scone. I was stress eating, but I couldn't stop myself. I didn't know what to make of my aunt's interaction with her new pet. However, the corgi behaved like a well-trained animal that had been with her for years, rather than a few months. I dismissed the thought. I didn't have time to dwell on the subject right now.

While we weren't quite running from the law, we certainly didn't want to be found—at least not yet. We needed evidence to point the finger at another suspect. Once found, and if we couldn't provide another suspect, we might find ourselves behind bars, relying on Evil Bun to catch the real killer. I shuddered at the thought. I had no expectations for a professional investigation.

"Is there someone we can talk to at this hour about Fiona?" I asked. "Someone close to her that could give us a clue?"

Aunt Coco's eyes brightened. "That's a brilliant idea. We can talk to Chrissy, Fiona's baker and assistant."

I checked the time. It was seven thirty in the morning. "Will she be awake at this time?"

"This is late for Chrissy. She's usually up at four thirty, getting the baking done before the coffee shop opens for the morning rush."

My jaw dropped. I didn't realize bakers had such an early morning shift, but it made sense now that I thought about it. Most pastries were eaten with the morning coffee. Oh, no. Did this mean we needed to wake up at the crack of dawn to open up the tea shop? After we got ourselves out of trouble with the law, I would need to sit down with my aunt to go through her expectations for the tea shop. It didn't sound like she had a business plan.

Aunt Coco marched along the sidewalk again,

and I trotted to keep up with her. We turned away from Old Town, heading deeper into the residential neighborhood. This part of town was mostly working-class folks. The homes were smaller and closer together, with multiple cars parked in the driveway and on the curbs. Maybe more than one family sharing a house together.

Fifteen minutes later, I was huffing and puffing. My aunt wasn't even breaking a sweat, and General trotted with his tongue hanging out, wagging his little fluffy butt. The two of them were having a grand old time while I was dying.

"Is this woman"—I inhaled to catch my breath—"the baker you're trying to steal from Fiona?"

Aunt Coco gave me a sideways glance. "Cedar Bear, you're out of shape, girl. We'll need to get you into an exercise program."

My aunt was right, but I wasn't going to give her the satisfaction. "I'll work on that later." It was the same comment that I had given her for the last decade, but maybe this time I might look into it. I took another deep breath. My lungs were now burning. "What were you and Fiona arguing about at the tea shop?"

Aunt Coco rolled her eyes. "Fiona took the entire conversation out of context and twisted it into something nefarious. I spoke to Chrissy Lane to ask where she went to culinary school, and if she knew any of her classmates who might be looking for a job. She knew we'd need a baker for the tea shop. And Fiona got all bent out of shape over this."

My ex-husband would consider this corporate espionage, trying to steal a business's secret weapon. And a baker was certainly part of the arsenal needed to make any business serving pastries a success. I could see why Fiona was upset. "From what Duncan said, it sounded like there was more history between the two of you."

"Fiona saw me as competition and used any excuse to call code enforcement or the police. It always turned out to be nothing, but it was still a pain for everyone involved."

"How long has this been going on?"

"Since I bought the building," Aunt Coco said.

"So, she's been harassing you for months?" I didn't bother hiding the surprise in my voice.

"Sounds about right." Aunt Coco frowned. "I guess I have gotten used to it."

"And no one spoke to Fiona about wasting everyone's time?"

"From what I gathered, Fiona's family runs this town," Aunt Coco said. "Her uncle is the mayor. And you met her nephew. Last year, another nephew tried to get rid of Everly so he could get the position. And they own about a third of the businesses in town. They have a lot of influence."

Unease settled into my stomach, churning with my scone. "Do you think they will pressure Chief Blunt to make a quick arrest?"

"Your guess is as good as mine," Aunt Coco said. For the first time, she appeared worried. Maybe it finally hit her that this was no game.

We arrived at a ranch house that had seen better days. The once white paint on the outside of the house had turned gray with weather and wear. The shingles were loose, and a patch of roof looked like it leaked. One cracked window pane was held together with duct tape. Overgrown grass creeped in from the sides on the narrow walkway to the house. Despite the crisp autumn air, there was an undercurrent of damp and mold.

I stared at the sad house for a long moment. But who was I to judge? It was still a step up from my apartment on top of the Vietnamese restaurant in San Jose.

"Chrissy came from money, but they lost it when she was a kid," Aunt Coco said. "It was about the time when the Spencers came into power in town.

Her family used to own that big mansion. The one that is now a bed and breakfast inn."

Aunt Coco squared her shoulders and marched up the steps. As I followed my aunt, I couldn't help but wonder if Chrissy Lane felt any resentment toward the Spencers. Reading between the lines, the Spencers might have something to do with the financial ruin of the Lane family.

## 7

## CHANEL WAS NUTS

The woman who opened the door was medium height, but busty with thick chestnut hair and blue eyes. She wore an oversized sweater and yoga pants. Her skin glistened like she'd just worked out, and her eyes seemed overly bright. Even though she wasn't in the kitchen, Chrissy Lane smelled of flour, sugar, and vanilla extract, like a pie fresh out of the oven.

"Coco, this isn't a good time," Chrissy said, leaning against the doorframe. "I have a stomach bug."

Aunt Coco grabbed Chrissy's hand, patting it. "Oh, sweetie. Do you need me to make you a cup of tea?"

And the next thing I knew, all three of us were in

the kitchen with Aunt Coco bustling around with the kettle and mugs. General sat on the floor next to me, his eyes closed. My aunt introduced me, but I didn't offer to shake hands because I didn't want the stomach bug. The last thing I needed was to get sick on top of everything.

Chrissy settled back into her chair, resigned. A few minutes later, all three of us were sitting around the kitchen table with steaming mugs of tea. Maybe this was how things were done in a small town, but I would have shut the door on my aunt's face.

"Have you seen the doctor, Chrissy?" Aunt Coco said. "Do you need anything else?"

Chrissy clutched her stomach. "Fiona's going to fire me. This is the second time I've called in sick this week."

Aunt Coco and I shared a look. My aunt raised an eyebrow, telling me to deliver the news. So, I had to play the bad cop.

I cleared my throat. "Were you sick yesterday morning too?"

Chrissy nodded. "There was no baking yesterday, and no baking today. It's the only thing keeping the coffee shop afloat." She lowered her voice even though there were just the three of us in the kitchen.

"Sometimes folks even skip the coffee and just buy the pastry." There was a hint of pride in her voice.

This explained why there were no customers yesterday morning at the coffee shop. And it also explained Fiona's over-the-top anger when she thought Aunt Coco was trying to steal her baker.

"Were you with anyone yesterday morning?" I asked.

Chrissy frowned. "No. I didn't feel well, so I slept in. And then I went to get something for my stomach at the drugstore. Your questions are starting to weird me out."

Not that I suspected the baker, but someone from the drugstore should be able to give her an alibi. "I'm sorry, but Fiona's dead."

Chrissy's face turned ashen. She jerked up from the chair, ran to the sink, and vomited. Aunt Coco rushed over and handed her some paper towels. Chrissy rinsed her mouth, and Aunt Coco helped the baker back into her chair.

"Sorry about that." Chrissy wiped her mouth. "Did you say Fiona's dead? What happened?"

I told her that Duncan found the body but kept out the detail about the hammer. After all, this might be something only the real killer would know.

Chrissy shook her head. "I don't believe this. There must be some kind of mistake."

"When was the last time you spoke to Fiona?" Aunt Coco asked.

"I don't remember," Chrissy said. "I left her a voicemail yesterday, and I got her voicemail again this morning."

"Do you have any idea who might want to kill Fiona?" I asked.

Chrissy shook her head. "She's not a bad boss. As long as I did the baking, she let me run the kitchen."

"Who would benefit from Fiona's death?" I asked.

Chrissy started to shake her head again and paused.

I leaned forward in my seat. "What about the husband? Do you know if there is a life insurance policy?"

"No insurance. Fiona gets money from a trust fund. The coffee shop is more of a hobby."

"If it's just a hobby, why is she harassing my aunt?" I asked.

"I never said she wasn't competitive," Chrissy said.

"Will Fiona's husband inherit the trust?"

"No, her son will."

"But the husband is probably the custodian, right?"

Chrissy chewed her lower lip for a long moment. "Now that Fiona is gone, this will become public knowledge soon enough. Duncan Spencer is the custodian."

My eyes widened. Fiona didn't trust her husband to manage the money for her son. And the money would go through her nephew instead—the nephew who was the first person at the crime scene. Now, this was interesting. Could he have killed his aunt and then cried wolf? "How was the marriage—"

Chrissy got up on shaky feet. "I'm sorry, but I'm not fit for company."

I felt horrible for intruding, but my curiosity was now piqued. I might never get another opportunity to get the inside scoop on Fiona. "One more ques— "

Chrissy made a barfing sound like she was about to throw up again.

I jumped to my feet, afraid I might get covered with vomit. "I hope you feel better soon."

At the door, Chrissy said, "What happens after this? Do I go to work tomorrow? Or am I unemployed?"

Aunt Coco patted Chrissy's shoulder. "Just get

better first, sweetie. If you need a job, you can come work at my tea shop."

Chrissy thanked my aunt and shut the door. We were back on the sidewalk. My aunt opened her mouth as if wanting to talk, but I shook my head. For all we knew, Chrissy could be behind the window watching us.

Once we were a block away, I turned to my aunt. "I can't believe you tried to hire Chrissy."

Aunt Coco shrugged. "Why wouldn't I? She's one of the best bakers in town."

"Fiona accused you of stealing her baker," I said. "Then Fiona died. And now you're offering her baker a job. Doesn't this sound suspicious to you?"

"That's ridiculous. People don't kill for an opportunity to hire an employee."

"But it'll still get you thrown in jail for a few days and have your neighbors pointing fingers at you."

Aunt Coco grew silent. She gazed down at General, cocking her head as if listening to something. "He just called me a birdbrain."

I glanced down at the corgi. His tongue was hanging out, and he regarded me with serene eyes. As long as we were on the same side, I guess it didn't matter for now if he was actually talking to my aunt or if her imagination was filling in the blanks.

I glanced at my watch. It was a little past eight. The whole morning stretched out in front of me. "Can we go back to the house, or do we continue to evade the police? Once Chief Blunt puts out the word that she is looking for us, someone will turn us in."

Aunt Coco cocked her head again, which appeared to be the sign that she was listening to her pet. General slowly blinked back at his owner. They were communicating with each other, but I didn't hear a sound. Telepathy? My aunt wasn't the woo-woo type who believed in spiritual energy. At least not the aunt I knew.

I shifted from foot to foot and yawned audibly. I needed coffee. A cup of tea in the morning wasn't enough caffeine. I probably needed to pick up a coffee maker and some beans. I shuddered at the thought of facing another morning with just a cup of black tea.

And yes, I was aware of the irony with my aunt opening a tea shop. Maybe I could convince her to turn it into a coffee and tea shop. No, I probably shouldn't even broach the idea until after Fiona's murderer was caught. It wouldn't look good for us otherwise.

"General thinks we should be in disguise," Aunt

Coco said, interrupting my thoughts.

I didn't like the sound of this. "People would think we're crazy for taking advice from a dog."

Aunt Coco linked her arm through mine, tugging me towards Old Town. "It's okay. They already think I'm nuts anyway. They call me 'Coconut' behind my back." She rolled her eyes. "I was named after Chanel. People these days don't have any fashion sense."

My gaze swept up and down my aunt. The velour tracksuit with white orthopedic shoes wasn't exactly the height of haute couture. I mumbled a sound that could be mistaken for agreement or anything else.

"I already ordered our Halloween costumes last month," Aunt Coco continued. "We might as well put them to use."

THE COSTUME SHOP was on a side street off of Main Street that the tourists usually didn't venture into. It was a little seedy, mainly because it was between a bar and a twenty-four-hour convenience store. It was a place for the locals. The costume shop's storefront windows were long and oval and the lettering on the glass read "Madden's Costume

Emporium and Taxidermy Shop" in gold and black letters.

"I'm not wearing anything from a taxidermy shop," I said. "The chemicals can seep into the fabric."

"Mary stuffs the animals out in her shed," Aunt Coco said. "It's just a business name."

I couldn't imagine why anyone thought a business name didn't matter. "Is this the only costume shop in town?"

"The only one in the entire county. There's always online shopping, but it would still take weeks to get here. And who wants to deal with returns if there is a sizing issue?"

"What do you mean? Isn't there two-day free shipping? Sometimes I can order something and get it within a few hours."

Aunt Coco stared at me like I was bonkers. "Not here. We don't have enough people for anyone to offer that kind of service."

I didn't know what to say. I knew the northern part of California wasn't as heavily populated as the southern part, but I didn't expect it to lack amenities. I checked my cell phone. Holy macaroni. There was no signal bar. I went back in time to the dinosaur days with my useless brick.

When Aunt Coco opened the entrance door, a bell above us rang, announcing our arrival. Costumes on hangers lined the shop's walls. Mannequins, each wearing a different costume, were scattered throughout the floor. The shop specialized in period costumes for women with more recent pop-culture costumes in the front for the Halloween crowd.

There was even a rack of evening and dinner gowns in the corner for the rare times someone needed to gussy up, although the styles were from the 80s. The air was heavy—a mixture of mothballs, dust, and rose paper. There was no sign of stuffed animals, which was a relief.

"Coco Chanel!" a woman called out from the cash register. She came over and gave my aunt a hug.

Aunt Coco introduced me to Mary Madden, the owner of the costume shop. She appeared to be in her mid-thirties and was a tall, slim woman with full cheeks and a button nose. She wore a high-neck nightgown with full sleeves. It was black and white with red lace trim. On top of the nightgown, she wore a red corset with black laces. Several golden chains draped around her neck. If this was her day wear, I wondered what she wore at night.

"Are the costumes ready?" Aunt Coco asked.

Mary grabbed two garment bags from the rack next to the dressing booth. "Do you want to try them on?"

"Yes, please." Aunt Coco opened and closed her hands in front of her like a child wanting a toy. "I've been waiting all year for this."

The two of them disappeared behind a dressing room. From the other side of the curtain, I heard the two women exclaiming over the costume. I didn't know what kind of disguise Mary had put together for us, but I had a feeling we would have to wear a wig. There weren't too many Asian women in town, and to blend in, we might have to go blonde. I wasn't looking forward to the itchy experience.

I slowly took a tour around the shop. The Japanese sword, mounted on the wall behind the cash register, looked authentic, but probably wasn't real. Wasn't it a hazard to have a real katana within reach when the general public came in and out of the shop?

In the back, there was an iridescent beaded curtain separating the back room from the retail space. "Can I use your restroom?"

"Through the beaded curtain, on your right," Mary called out from behind the dressing booth.

I followed Mary's instructions and took care of

business. My gaze swept through the storage space. The metal door in front of me was probably a back door. Next to it was a large whiteboard with numbers and dates on it. I took a step closer. It was some kind of inventory count. On the corner, Mary taped a photo—the instant-develop kind that was faded and blurry. I bent closer and peered at it. It was a younger Mary with a dark-haired Hispanic man. They were holding their hands out toward the camera lens so it focused on the glittering diamond ring on her hand.

I straightened and left the back room. I wasn't jealous that Mary was in a happy marriage. I was once just as starry-eyed. I just couldn't be around happily married couples at the moment.

When Aunt Coco came out of the dressing booth, my jaw dropped. My aunt had completely transformed her appearance with an orange wig, top hat with mini teacups on the brim, and royal blue velvet dinner jacket. She looked like an overweight Mad Hatter.

Even General had swapped out his green beret for bunny ears and the rhinestone bowtie on his collar twinkled under the fluorescent light. What happened to going under the radar? Everyone would stare at us and think we were insane. Even though it was the first week of October, it was too early for dressing up.

My gaze swiveled to the costume in Mary's hand. Holy macaroni. My aunt must be smoking something to think I would walk around as Alice. "I thought we were going undercover. How will these costumes help us to blend in?"

"Who said anything about blending in?" Aunt Coco said. "We will hide in plain sight. Besides, we want as many people to see us in costume as possible."

"Why?" I asked. Did my aunt want to go to jail in style? Did she want us to be known as the Wonderland Murderers?

"The residents get to vote for the best costume at the annual Halloween block party in Old Town. And the more people who associate us with a tea party, the better." Aunt Coco fluffed out her orange wig. "The tea shop is opening next month. This will help get the word out."

Mary handed me the costume. The blue dress had puffy sleeves, a fitted waist, and a flared skirt. A clear plastic bag held the white apron, white tights, black Mary Jane shoes, and blonde wig. I knew there would be a wig.

"I'm not wearing this," I said, crossing my arms.

"All you have to do is stand next to me," Aunt Coco said. "We need an Alice to complete our family theme. You don't even need to say any lines."

I shook my head. Wasn't there a pecking order in jail? I was willing to bet my rope soap that Alice was as low as one could go in that pecking order. I could imagine Evil Bun's laughter as she slammed the door shut and threw away the key. "What about Josh? Doesn't he have to dress up too?" If I had to make a fool of myself, my brother wasn't getting out of it.

"Josh is going to be the dormouse," Aunt Coco said.

I couldn't believe my aunt said that with a straight face. How could my six-foot tall brother be a tiny mouse? Maybe that was part of the irony. "Forget about the costume contest or the family theme. We have bigger things to worry about—like staying out of jail."

"This is all part of the plan, Cedar Bear," Aunt Coco said. "Now go change."

I shook my head. "I still don't get it."

"People will stop and talk to us. And some people will want to take pictures with us, which is another opportunity to get them to talk."

"You lost me. Why do I care if random people talk to me?"

"If people don't talk to us, how are we going to investigate this murder case?"

Mary's eyes widened, and she lowered her voice even though there was no one else in the shop. "I heard that Malcolm Spencer was looking for you, Coco."

"Who is Malcolm? Fiona's husband?" I asked.

I was curious about Fiona's marriage and how her nephew ended up as the custodian of her son's trust.

"Her father," Mary said and shuddered.

There was something about the tone that alerted my internal antenna. Mary didn't want to talk about Malcolm, which made me want to talk about him.

"Why is he looking for me?" Aunt Coco said.

Mary shrugged. "Malcolm told Chief Blunt that if she doesn't find the killer, then he'll have to take care of it himself. He said someone would end up at the bottom of Trinity Lake."

## 8

## MISTAKES WERE MADE

"I know he's upset about his daughter," Aunt Coco said. "But I don't think he'll do anything. Malcolm is a big talker, but he's not a criminal."

"He means it this time," Mary said. "Fiona was his only daughter. He had two sons, but he lost them both. No one really knew what happened." She shrugged. "You would think with all the women he ran around with, he would have more children. But nope. He only got Fiona now. And she was daddy's little girl. She was supposed to inherit everything, but now the money will go to her son."

"We heard that Duncan was the custodian of the son's trust. Why do you think her husband isn't managing the money?" I asked.

"Fiona's money came from her daddy, and he ain't giving it to Juan Perez," Mary said. "But letting Duncan manage the money is a stupid idea. He already blew through his own trust fund in less than five years."

"Duncan was a trust fund baby?" I asked.

Mary nodded with a wide grin. "Gambling. He used to go down to Vegas several times a year like he was a high roller."

"What happened when the money ran out?" I asked.

"He started borrowing it. He robbed Peter to pay Paul. And this went on for about a year until the loan sharks showed up in town. That was exciting," Mary said.

Aunt Coco rubbed her hands together. "This is better than *General Hospital*."

"And then what?" I asked.

"Malcolm rescued him," Mary said. "His grand-daddy paid off all his debts and told Duncan to get a job."

"How do you know Malcolm is looking for me?" Aunt Coco said.

"His goon came around this morning," Mary said. "I watched him go from shop to shop."

A chill ran down my spine. I didn't like the sound

of this. What were we truly up against? Was Evil Bun the least of our worries? What if Malcolm Spencer lashed out at anyone who might be a suspect? I had to solve this case before my aunt got into more trouble.

Aunt Coco shoved the costume into my hands and gave me puppy eyes. "I had a rough morning. If we're in costume, it would cheer me up. If nothing else, it would be nice to win the costume contest for a change. And you probably would not see anyone you know."

I grumbled under my breath but went into the dressing booth. How could I say no to the mother who raised me? "I got that Malcolm Spencer is Fiona's father. But what does he do? Why are people afraid of him?"

"Malcolm is an enigma," Mary said. "No one knows what he does for a living. He has never been caught doing anything, but everyone is afraid of him. My mom said he came to town one day forty years ago, and the next thing we knew, the Spencers were running the town. He's like the Godfather of Mirror Falls."

I slipped off my boots. "I find it hard to believe there is organized crime here."

"Who knows what's coming in from Canada

these days?" Aunt Coco said. "It's a straight shot through town, and then down south to San Francisco and Los Angeles."

I peeled off my sweatpants and T-shirt and pulled on the tights. They were scratchy, like a bad wool sweater, but they were as warm as my sweatpants.

The rumors about Malcolm Spencer were probably stories the locals made up about an outsider who had money and influence. While I doubted there was a crime boss in town, I still didn't like the idea of having another potential enemy at our back.

"Maybe we should offer our condolences to Malcolm," Aunt Coco said.

Mary gasped. "Do you want to end up at the bottom of the lake, Coco?"

"I think Malcolm is sweet on me," Aunt Coco said, ignoring her friend's comment.

"Here we go again," Mary mumbled under her breath.

Aunt Coco launched into a tale about her meeting with Malcolm at the waffle house. "I was building a waffle tower when Malcolm came over and offered me toothpicks to help keep the waffles together. When we reached for the toothpicks at the same time, our hands touched." My aunt sighed.

"We spent a fantastic two hours together before I had to leave to meet with the contractor."

Something about my aunt's story sounded very familiar to me. However, this was the first time I heard of the date with Malcolm Spencer. When did my aunt start dating again? With her attachment to General, I thought she was still too hung up on my uncle's death to look at another man.

I tugged the dress over my head. It was loose, probably because my aunt bought the size I had been when she'd last seen me. It was better than being too tight.

I put on the blonde wig and checked myself out in the full-length mirror. Not bad. Someone would have to do a double take to recognize me. Maybe my aunt was right. Hiding in plain sight wasn't a bad plan.

I stepped out of the dressing booth and held both hands up in the air. I did a slow spin to show off my costume. If I had to put in the effort, I might as well have a little fun with it.

Aunt Coco clapped. "Cedar Bear, you look lovely. No one will recognize us."

General gave me a small bark and wagged his tail, approving the costume.

"Everyone will recognize General," I said.

"Not a problem," Aunt Coco said. "We'll leave him with Babcia. She has a dachshund, and the two of them are friends. What do you think of my idea about talking to Malcolm?"

"I think you're nuts," Mary said.

"I'm not asking you," Aunt Coco said. "And don't you go around telling people we're investigating Fiona's death."

Mary mimed zipping up her lips. "I won't breathe a word to anyone, except for our sisters in the Survivors Club."

I felt a moment of shame for my earlier flash of jealousy toward Mary's marriage. I didn't realize she was a widow. The Survivors Club was my aunt's self-help book club, and the ladies in it would have lost someone to be a member.

Aunt Coco had joined the book club a year ago and often mentioned them in our phone conversations. I didn't think this would automatically put them in the circle of trust, but my aunt was more trusting than me.

"I guess that would be alright," Aunt Coco said.

"Maybe we should check on Fiona's husband," I said. "Isn't it a small town thing for the church ladies to bring over a casserole or mac and cheese?"

Aunt Coco and Mary looked at each other and

burst out laughing. With his tongue hanging out, even General looked as if he was amused.

When the laughter died down, I asked, "Was that a city yuppie comment?"

Mary nodded. "At least you are aware of your shortcomings. And no, the church ladies around here don't show up with a casserole to solve all the problems in this town. Besides, the Spencers are outsiders."

I wasn't sure what to make of the comment. The Spencers had been in town for the last forty years. How were they still outsiders? I glanced at my aunt. "You've only been in town for two years. And I only lived here for the first decade of my life. I guess we're both outsiders, too?"

Mary shook her head. "Oh, no. Both of you are one of us. Coco married one of the Woods boys. And the Woods had been here since Mirror Falls was a logging camp."

I got a warm, tingly sensation on my chest. It was good to know we were part of the community, even if it was by proxy through our family connections. "Aunt Coco, is your contractor working at the tea shop today?"

Aunt Coco slapped her forehead. "I clean forgot all about him." She pulled out her cell phone and tapped on the screen. After several seconds, she left a message for him on his voicemail.

"After he sees the crime scene tape, he should be smart enough to call you back," I said.

Mary and Aunt Coco shared a look.

"I wouldn't be so sure about that," Mary muttered under her breath.

"Kelly's tools are sharper than him," Aunt Coco said.

I didn't like the sound of this. Were we looking at a half-finished tea shop like my aunt's kitchen? "Let's go check on the tea shop."

Surely the contractor would be smart enough to ask a few questions at the sight of the crime scene tape. Checking on the tea shop was for my peace of mind more than anything else. But maybe we could find a clue about Fiona's killer. We didn't have time to look around yesterday before Chief Blunt decided the tea shop was a crime scene.

A FEW MINUTES LATER, we were out of the costume shop, strolling toward Main Street. Aunt Coco wore her top hat at a jaunty angle and sauntered like she was in a parade, waving to anyone who glanced in her direction. Even General pranced, wagging his fluffy little butt. The dog was too cute. How could he be my uncle's reincarnated spirit? My uncle never pranced in his life. People said that General Gabriel Woods was authoritative, bold, and resourceful. No one had ever called him cute—not even his mother.

Someone whistled at us from across the street. "Looking good, Coco!"

Aunt Coco gave him two thumbs up. General gave him a friendly bark.

I rolled my eyes. So much for a disguise.

"Alice, you're hot!" the man continued.

My cheeks burned at the attention, and I averted my gaze, not quite sure how to respond to the comment. With my oversize winter parka that went to mid-thigh, he only saw the bottom half of the blue skirt and the white tights. He was probably being polite.

My stomach rumbled. It was still too early for lunch, but I wouldn't say no to a sandwich. For the first time since I became an adult, I had lost the extra padding that always made me the chubby best friend. This was the only upside to my divorce. And since I got a "do-over" on the weight department, I was never dieting again.

The yellow crime scene tape across the coffee

shop and tea shop could be seen from half a block away. I looked around, but didn't see Evil Bun or her minions. The townsfolk went about their business, though I was sure Fiona's death was the talk around the water cooler. For this time of year there were a few tourists shopping, though the summer crowd was gone. But there were still too many witnesses for us to walk in through the front door with the yellow crime scene tape. Someone might call the cops on us.

"We'll need to go in through the back alley," I said.

From the entrance of the back alley, I saw a man unloading an air compressor from a pickup truck next to the back door of the tea shop. One side of the crime scene tape was removed and flapped in the breeze.

"Kelly," Aunt Coco yelled. "What are you doing?" She ran up to the truck and gestured at the crime scene tape.

Kelly Hammer was short for his given profession. He was about two hundred fifty pounds, balding, and had a bushy mustache that made him look like Mario from the *Super Mario* video game. Though his clothes were too tight around his girth, he moved with ease like he had hidden muscle beneath the padding.

Another man came out of the tea shop to grab something from the truck. He was tall, lanky, and also had a bushy mustache. When he stood next to Kelly, I couldn't help but think that he looked like Luigi. Holy macaroni. My aunt had hired the Super Mario brothers.

Kelly squinted at my aunt's face for a long moment. "Coco, is that you?"

I had forgotten that we were in costumes. Alice and the Mad Hatter versus the Super Mario brothers in a back alley. I suppressed the urge to laugh.

"Didn't you see the crime scene tape?" Aunt Coco said.

"We haven't even finished remodeling the tea shop yet," Kelly said. "It's too early to start decorating for Halloween. Or to walk around in costumes."

"Are you for real? Didn't you see the bloody fingerprint on the door handle?" Aunt Coco said.

"Which is wasted here on the back door," Kelly said. "You need to put the bloody fingerprint on the front door."

"This is no decoration, you nincompoop," Aunt Coco said, hands on her hips. "The tea shop is a crime scene. Geez, man, you need to keep up with the rumors around town."

Kelly crossed his arms. "I don't appreciate the way you're talking to me, Coco. I took on this job as a favor to Gabriel. If you don't like how I do things around here, maybe you should go find yourself another contractor."

"Whoa." I made the time-out sign with my hands. "Let's everybody take a deep breath and restart this conversation." We were not going to be stuck with a half-finished tea shop. I held out my hand to the contractor. "Hi, I am Cedar Woods. Coco's niece."

Kelly shook my hand reluctantly. The tall man introduced himself, and I immediately forgot his name. My mind still labeled him as Luigi.

"That's no decoration," I said, gesturing at the back door. "Chief Blunt put the crime scene tape up yesterday. Fiona Spencer was murdered."

"So, you finally got fed up with Fiona," Kelly said. "A smart person would take care of it elsewhere."

"I didn't do it," Aunt Coco said.

"I was wondering about the crime scene tape at the coffee shop," Luigi said. "I thought the two of them were competing over the Halloween decorations. They compete over everything."

"I wish it was a Halloween decoration." I gave my aunt a sideways glance. She had never mentioned competing with Fiona. "And apparently, the killer decided to smear a bloody fingerprint on the tea shop's back door while making a getaway."

"I hope Everly got what she needed because that fingerprint is long gone," Kelly said. "And here I thought it was just Coco being cuckoo."

"I don't think we can resume work until Chief Blunt removes the crime scene tape," I said.

"When is she planning to let us get back to work?" Kelly asked. "This will put us behind schedule for our other jobs."

"We don't know," I said. "I guess it depends on how long it'll take for her to find Fiona's killer."

"I bet it's the husband," Kelly said. "I saw him lurking back here yesterday morning."

"I thought you were at a different job," I said.

"When I got there, I realized I left the air compressor at the tea shop," Kelly said. "So I turned around to get it."

"What time was this?" I asked.

"Eight," Kelly said. "I remember the time

because it was a late start. I saw Juan Perez getting into a white cargo van."

Kelly and his assistant went inside the tea shop to gather up their tools. As they got into the pickup truck, he said, "Have you seen my hammer?"

Aunt Coco and I shared a look.

I gave Kelly my best innocent look. "I'll keep an eye out for it."

"If I can't resume work by the end of the week, I'm moving onto my next job." Kelly started the engine. "We can't sit around and wait. I've got to keep my guys busy. You'll have to wait until after the New Year to get back on my schedule."

My heart sank at the contractor's parting words. I didn't think helping my aunt start her small business would be a piece of cake, but neither did I expect it to be mission impossible. At the rate things were going, she might end up in jail and destitute. And it would be all my fault. Why did I pick up the hammer in the first place?

# 9

# UNEASY ALIBIS

I studied the back door of the tea shop. It was a typical metal door with a bar across the middle with a kickstand at the bottom. Pushing the bar unlocked the door from the inside.

"How did the killer get inside the tea shop?" I asked. "Wasn't the door locked?"

Aunt Coco averted her gaze, choosing to address the overcast sky. "I might have left the door propped open."

"Why?"

"The HVAC isn't working properly, and it was stuffy inside."

Like my decision to pick up the hammer, this simple action led to our current predicament. Unfortunately, there was no other clue on the door. The contractor and his laborer had rubbed off the bloody fingerprint. How were we going to explain this to the police?

We strode over to the coffee shop's back door. Aunt Coco reached for the handle, and I grabbed her hand.

"Wait." I peered at the door handle but didn't see any visible fingerprints.

The killer was careful enough to keep his or her bloody hand off the door handle here, but left behind a smeared fingerprint at the door handle for the tea shop. The setup was comically stupid, but it could land my aunt in jail. If only I could trust Evil Bun to conduct a professional investigation.

"Should we take a look inside?" Aunt Coco asked.

I shook my head. As much as I wanted to look around, I knew we shouldn't contaminate the crime scene further.

I put on my gloves, and we locked up the tea shop. Though the crime scene was contaminated beyond repair, it felt right not to leave fresh fingerprints behind. I tried attaching the crime scene tape across the door again, but Kelly must have done something to the adhesive because it wouldn't stick. So, we left the yellow tape flapping in the wind.

I yawned. The breakfast tea wasn't strong enough for my taste. I should probably purchase a coffee maker. As much as I loved my aunt, her idea of coffee was the icky instant stuff. And I couldn't afford the fancy coffees from the coffee shop every morning. "I could use a cup of joe."

Aunt Coco led us out of the alley and back onto the boardwalk in front of the shops. As we approached the lumber pile, the corner of a white sheet of paper fluttered in the wind. "Why didn't we ask Kelly to move the lumber?"

I'd forgotten all about the lumber delivery. It seemed so long ago, and given the events of the last few hours, such a minor inconvenience.

Aunt Coco stepped off the boardwalk and onto the street. She pulled the sheet of paper off. "Seriously? I can't believe Duncan Spencer gave me a citation. His aunt just died. Why is he even working?"

The corner of my mouth twitched, and I suppressed the urge to smile. Only my aunt would think she should benefit from her rival's death. "How much is the fee?"

"Twenty-five dollars a day."

I grimaced. "We're at fifty dollars already. It will be seventy-five dollars tomorrow."

Aunt Coco whipped out her phone. "I better call Luke. He can move the lumber to the back alley."

I was surprised Luke was available at my aunt's beck and call. "Doesn't he have a job?"

"Luke owns the sawmill. He doesn't work traditional hours like everyone else." Aunt Coco returned to her cell phone, tapping out a message. She pocketed her cell phone. "Let's go have lunch with Babcia."

My stomach rumbled at the thought of food. "We should take care of the citation first. What if there are penalties in addition to the fines?"

"Can't the citation wait?" Aunt Coco said.

I shook my head. As much as I would love a filling meal, time was of the essence when it came to an investigation, according to my brother, who was a Sherlock Holmes fan. "It's an excuse to talk to Duncan."

Aunt Coco led the way toward Town Hall.

"Are Luke and Josh in a relationship?" I asked.

Aunt Coco gave me a sideways glance. "Why? Are you interested?"

I pretended to shrug nonchalantly. "I'm trying to figure out if he is friend or foe."

"Definitely a friend, and definitely not gay."

"He may be your friend, but he's certainly not mine."

Aunt Coco chuckled. "It's kind of strange the two of you didn't get off to a good start."

I waited for a long moment, but Aunt Coco didn't appear to be in a gossipy mood. I wasn't giving my aunt satisfaction by asking about this "definite friend." "How come you didn't get the lumber from Luke in the first place?"

Aunt Coco rolled her eyes. "It's all Kelly's fault. He has something against Luke. Wouldn't use his lumber for any jobs."

"Luke mentioned that you signed the contract with Kelly before he could look it over."

Aunt Coco pointed at the corgi. "General rushed me into signing the contract. It's all his fault."

The dog wagged his tail at me, and I petted him on the head. "You're blaming the dog?"

"He has to take personal responsibility for his actions."

I burst out laughing. My aunt looked at me like I was soft in the head, which made me laugh harder.

Town Hall was a two-story brick building with a grassy square in front and a giant red rabbit sculpture in the middle. There were folks hurrying to and from the court house on the right.

Aunt Coco led us to a side entrance in Town Hall, away from the police station next door. I was disturbed that my aunt knew how to skulk around undetected.

The inside was brightly lit by several large windows. It was bigger on the inside than it looked from the outside. A sweeping stairway led up to the second floor. On the left, a set of double doors led to the chamber room where the mayor and town council had their public meetings. In front of us were a dozen closed doors with plastic signs of the various government departments. At the end of the hall was a counter for folks to access public services.

Aunt Coco marched up to the counter and rang the bell. The door behind the counter opened, and a woman came out.

"Can I help you?" the woman asked.

"It's me. Coco Woods," Aunt Coco said.

The woman studied Aunt Coco's face. "For a second, I thought the circus came to town."

My aunt gave the woman a deadpan expression. She wasn't amused.

The woman picked up the phone that was behind the counter. "Are you here to see Duncan again?"

"Lucky me." Aunt Coco waved the citation in the air. "I got another one."

The woman punched in a number, spoke on the phone, and hung up. "He's coming." She went back through the door, and we were left alone again.

Duncan came out shortly, wearing his lanyard name badge and holding his clipboard. The fluorescent light highlighted the eye bags underneath his brown eyes. His slumped shoulders no longer held the air of confidence of yesterday. His grim expression didn't look like someone expecting a big payday. But then again, this could be an act.

"Coco, are you here to pay the fine?" Duncan asked.

He didn't appear surprised at Aunt Coco's costume. I wondered if his coworker had warned him or if dressing up was part of my aunt's routine.

Aunt Coco waved the citation. "I challenge the citation."

Duncan rubbed his temples. "Does the pile of lumber in front of the tea shop belong to you?"

Aunt Coco nodded.

"Is it blocking several parking spaces?" Duncan asked.

Aunt Coco nodded again.

"Then I don't see how you can challenge the citation," Duncan said.

"But your aunt just died," Aunt Coco said.

"I don't get your point," Duncan said.

"Why are you even working?" Aunt Coco asked. "Shouldn't you be home grieving?"

"I don't want to be home thinking about the horrible scene," Duncan said curtly.

"But if you were home, then this citation wouldn't have happened." Aunt Coco slapped the sheet of paper onto the counter. "I rest my case."

Duncan glanced at me and swiveled his gaze to my aunt and back to me again like he expected me to do something about her.

I could see my aunt's logic, but if Duncan weren't at work, another code enforcement person would probably give my aunt the same citation. But since the murder suspect looked as if he wanted me to rescue the conversation, I had to do my duty as a Good Samaritan.

"I'm sorry about your aunt." I caught Duncan's warning look, but beggars couldn't be choosers. We were still the only ones in the public space of Town Hall, but who knew how long we would have this privacy? "Who do you think killed her?"

Duncan stiffened. "If you want to contest the

citation, you can fill out a form and have my supervisor review it." He pulled a form from the compartment on his clipboard and slid it across the counter.

Aunt Coco snatched up the form. "I will contest this citation." She glanced at me and then at the paper.

I blinked back at her. Message received. We didn't have a lot of time left to question Duncan. As my aunt began filling out the form, taking her time to form the letters with her handwriting, I decided to switch tactics with my questions. If friendly didn't work, I should get straight to the point, and maybe shock would get Duncan to spill the beans.

"We heard you will be the custodian of your nephew's trust fund," I said.

Duncan ignored my comment and focused his attention on the form.

"This gives you the perfect motive to kill Fiona," I said.

Duncan's head jerked up and met my gaze. "I did not kill my aunt," he said through gritted teeth.

He sounded like this wasn't the first time he had to defend himself. Interesting.

"You could have killed her and then cried wolf," Aunt Coco said, glancing up from the form. "It's not uncommon for the killer to be the one to discover the victim."

"And you have a gambling problem," I said. "You blew through your own trust fund, so it's not a stretch to think you want to dip into Fiona's son's trust fund."

"Have you told anyone about this?" Duncan whispered.

I shrugged. "We don't need to tell anyone. Think about what the professionals would find." It took all my willpower to keep my game face on at the thought of Evil Bun putting together a professional investigation. "I assume you visited the coffee shop regularly, so your DNA is probably all over the crime scene."

"It's not me," Duncan said.

"Then who?" I said.

Aunt Coco resumed filling out the form and sang under her breath, "Who stole the cookie from the cookie jar?"

I cleared my throat. Seriously? My aunt couldn't wait until we were done questioning Duncan.

Aunt Coco pointed at General. "He started it."

I ignored my aunt's comment and returned my attention to Duncan. "If it's not you, who would have a motive for killing Fiona?"

Duncan scowled at my aunt. "Why did you have to kill my aunt, Coco? I know she wasn't easy to get along with, but you didn't have to kill her."

I bristled at his words. Holy macaroni. He was trying to shift the blame. "My aunt has an alibi at the time of Fiona's death."

"You don't count," Duncan said.

"Actually, you are her alibi," I said.

"What are you talking about?" he said.

"Where were you when you answered Fiona's call?" I said.

"Here in the office. She called through the main line. Even though we're family, I still need to log her call."

"My aunt was outside yelling at the delivery truck driver when Fiona said she was calling code enforcement. What time did she call you?" I said.

"I don't remember," he said.

"Can you check the call history on your cell phone?"

Duncan pulled his phone from his back pocket. "9:45 AM."

"How long did that conversation last?" I asked.

Duncan checked his phone again. "About four minutes. I tried to convince Aunt Fiona that it wasn't a big deal to block a few parking spots on a weekday for a few hours. It isn't the tourist season."

"Assuming Fiona called the police immediately after talking to you, and the conversation lasted for the same duration, Fiona was still alive at about 9:50 AM, maybe 9:55 AM."

"I still don't understand what you're getting at," Duncan said.

"During this time, my aunt was talking to Luke Kai on her cell phone about moving the lumber pile," I said. "When she finished with the call, you showed up. And you were with us until you walked inside the coffee shop and discovered Fiona's body. So the two of you are alibis for each other."

Duncan gaped at me. "Are you saying that someone killed my aunt while we were talking on the street?"

I nodded. "The timing seems about right. You probably missed the killer by minutes."

Duncan shook his head. "As much as I would like to believe you, all the evidence points to Coco."

"My aunt had no reason to kill Fiona."

"I have been dealing with these two for months. We have records of all the times Aunt Fiona had called code enforcement or the police's office."

Duncan's gaze shifted to my aunt. "Did you get fed up and snap?"

"If it were me, I wouldn't get caught," Aunt Coco said.

Duncan raised an eyebrow. "I rest my case."

"What will happen to your aunt's coffee shop?" I asked. "Who will inherit it?"

"That's a crass question," Duncan said.

"If Fiona doesn't trust her husband to look after their son's money, then she isn't leaving him anything," I said. "You're getting the coffee shop, aren't you?"

"I can't help it if my aunt loved and trusted me."

"And I hope the trust isn't misplaced," I said. "However, it still makes you look guilty. In situations like this, the police would follow the money trail to see who would benefit from the murder."

Duncan grimaced. It looked as if he had thought of all this already. "What do you want from me?"

"Who else would benefit from Fiona's death?" I asked again.

"My aunt's husband, Juan Perez."

"How?" I asked.

"Freedom."

I blinked. I hadn't expected this answer. "What do you mean?"

"Nobody leaves Malcolm Spencer's daughter," Duncan said. "Until Fiona was done with the marriage, Juan had no choice but to stay."

"What do you think of your aunt's relationship with her husband? Were they happy together?" I asked.

Duncan shrugged. "They were like any old married couple—boring."

"Who was your aunt having an affair with?" I asked, changing the subject.

"What are you talking about?" Duncan asked.

"Everyone said Juan was a long-suffering husband for putting up with your aunt's infidelity."

Duncan's gaze swiveled to my aunt. "Have you been spreading rumors about my aunt? That's slander. If you're looking for a suspect, you should investigate Juan. He wasn't a model husband."

"What do you mean?" Aunt Coco said.

"I'm not the one playing detective. If I were you, I would be careful where you stick your nose." Duncan snatched the form from the counter, spun on his heels, and headed toward the door. "Coco, you know the drill. My supervisor will give you a call." The door slammed shut.

## 10

## THE GESTAPO

As we strolled—actually, Aunt Coco scurried from tree to tree like she was a nefarious villain—back to the alley behind my aunt's house, I considered our next move. I wasn't sure if Chief Blunt was still searching the neighborhood for us, but I didn't want to take any chances of running into her. Disguise or no disguise, we stood out, especially with General wearing bunny ears.

"What do you think about Duncan's reaction to your questions?" Aunt Coco said. "Is he still at the top of your suspects list?"

"He's the most obvious suspect." I ticked off the points with my fingers. "Gambling habit. Access to a trust fund." I frowned. "But we're his alibi. He only disappeared from our view for a few minutes."

"But what if he killed Fiona, made his getaway through the back alley, and then came back around to the front to harass us about the lumber pile?"

"There's still not enough time," I said. "He was in the office when he took the call. Then he drove to the tea shop. He would need another five minutes to kill Fiona."

Aunt Coco looked disappointed. "Oh."

"Also, the murderer isn't stupid," I said. "And having the most obvious motive is stupid."

"What do we do now?" Aunt Coco said. "Quite a few people know we are investigating this murder."

Up until now, I hadn't thought about what would happen if the killer knew we were asking questions. It had seemed like a little fun diversion. "First, we stick together. This way it would be two against one."

Aunt Coco nodded. "And we have General. He wouldn't let anyone harm us."

I glanced down at the corgi, prancing happily next to my aunt. A well-aimed kick would probably take him out. He was more of a liability than protection.

I reviewed my conversation with the code enforcement officer. "Duncan said that Juan would gain his freedom with Fiona's death. By all accounts, he had put up with Fiona's infidelity for years and the underlying threat from his father-in-law. Why does he need his freedom now?"

Aunt Coco shrugged.

"Who was Fiona having an affair with?" I said. "We should talk to her lover. Maybe he knows who wanted to kill her."

"That's a good question. I had never seen Fiona with another man. She was discreet," Aunt Coco said.

"Let's ask around and see if we can get a name. Someone would have known about the affair, seen the two of them together. There was only one affair, right?"

"I haven't been part of the community long enough to know," Aunt Coco said. "Let me ask Babcia. She knows everything that goes on in this town." She handed me the leash and pulled out her cell phone.

As Aunt Coco tapped out a message, my thoughts drifted to the device in my purse. It was a sad state of affairs that I didn't even have a working cell phone. Even at the lowest point of my divorce, I had access to the Internet and the folks in my contacts list.

Aunt Coco's cell phone dinged with an incoming text message. "Babcia doesn't know who Fiona's lover is. Now that's strange." She slipped the device back into her pocket.

"Who mentioned Fiona was having an affair?" I asked.

Aunt Coco blinked at my question. "Why, it is common knowledge."

Even though I didn't like Fiona for the way she had treated my aunt, I wondered if this common knowledge was a rumor put forth by her killer. But this implied someone who had been plotting this murder for a while.

I shivered at the thought. A crime of passion was much easier to understand. A planned murder for months and years in the making was too frightening. It meant this person had patience and cunning.

Aunt Coco's cell phone dinged again. She checked her message. "Josh is freaking out because he can't get in touch with you."

I told my aunt about the lack of cell phone reception.

Aunt Coco tapped a message to my brother and put her device away again. "Why didn't you say something earlier? Now we need to double back to the phone store."

"How many times have we gone back to Old Town today? At this rate, we have walked a dozen miles."

Aunt Coco checked her smartwatch. "Just seven. And it's not that bad. When you add in my walk this morning, I already walked ten miles, and I'm not even complaining yet."

"Let's deal with this tomorrow." I couldn't take another trek back to Old Town. "I need to gather my thoughts and think through what we learned today." I rubbed my chin. "I probably should write things down in a notebook."

Aunt Coco wiggled her cell phone in the air. "There's an app for that. And you can zoom in, so you don't need your reading glasses."

My aunt had a point, but I bet the phone would die on me when I needed to access the information.

"Will contesting the citation make a difference?" I asked.

"Nah," Aunt Coco said. "I'll end up having to pay the fine. Just like all the other times, but it's fun to get under Duncan's skin. He deserves it for pandering to Fiona's wild speculations."

As I approached my aunt's street, a sense of unease washed over me. Not surprisingly, a police cruiser was parked in front of the house. But something about the white cargo van parked at the alley's entrance seemed off. Was it the tinted windows? Or the dent in the rear bumper?

I squinted at the van but couldn't make out anything. Acting on instinct, I pulled my aunt behind a Douglas fir and whispered, "Something's wrong."

"What is it?" my aunt whispered back.

I didn't like the hint of excitement in her voice. Aunt Coco was having entirely too much fun, and this worried me. Maybe she thought this was all a game, as I did when we had left the house this morning. Now I was concerned we might be out of our league.

"Someone is watching the house," I said. Who owned a white cargo van? My mind raced as I tried to remember who had mentioned the van before, but the information eluded me.

"I can see the cop car," Aunt Coco said. "We can use the back alley again."

I pointed at the van. "I'm more concerned with who is inside that vehicle."

"It's probably just someone from the neighborhood," Aunt Coco said.

My gaze swiveled between the police cruiser and the white cargo van. My gut told me the van wasn't a random car from the neighborhood. I couldn't shake the feeling that something dangerous lurked inside the van. "Does Babcia have a car?"

Aunt Coco nodded. "Why?"

"I think we should double back a couple of blocks and have Babcia pick us up from there. Tell her to bring blankets so we can hide underneath them in the backseat. And then she'll have to drive straight into her garage when we get back."

"This feels like a spy movie." Aunt Coco's eyes gleamed, and she rubbed her hands together in glee. "I can be Agent 007. No, maybe Agent 009. And you can be Agent 008. Yes, then we can both get lucky."

"Do the numbers mean anything?" I asked.

"In Chinese culture, the number nine is favored by couples or the elderly for its association with longevity. And the number eight in Chinese is a homonym for wealth."

It made sense my aunt wanted code names that would bring us what we needed—longevity for her and wealth for me.

I didn't know if Aunt Coco believed we needed to be careful or if we were role-playing. However, she followed my instructions and spoke to Babcia on the phone. While my aunt talked to her friend, we retraced our steps until we were a couple of blocks away.

A few minutes later, Babcia arrived to pick us up, rolling down the street at fifteen miles an hour. Holy macaroni. I had forgotten about the cataract. With Babcia's face pressed close to the steering wheel, I was afraid the airbag might take out her remaining good eye.

Halina Nowak was known as Babcia in town, which was Polish for grandma. My Chinese aunt and her friend were a study in contrasts. While my aunt was short and round, her friend was tall and thin. Babcia's face was a map of wrinkles with a cataract creeping into one blue eye. Her hair was completely white, with a patch missing around her temples. I liked that she didn't even bother hiding the patch behind a hair clip or bow. If my aunt reminded me of a human version of the BB8 droid from Star Wars, then Babcia was C-3PO.

Aunt Coco and I piled into the car and huddled in the backseat. Babcia threw a smelly blanket over us and got back on the road. I breathed through my mouth so I wouldn't gag. The smell didn't seem to bother my aunt or the dog. As we drove back to Babcia's house, I couldn't help but smile at the absurdity of the situation. We weren't even officially murder suspects yet, but we certainly were acting like fugitives.

Babcia pressed the garage remote, and the door rattled up in its tracks. "Almost on the home stretch. We are passing the police cruiser."

I held my breath. Babcia was just a neighbor returning from an errand. No reason for the police to stop her.

Babcia pulled into her driveway. "Everly is getting out of her car. Maybe I can make it inside."

"Too suspicious," Aunt Coco whispered. "Just get rid of her."

My heart pounded in my chest, and I peered through a gap in the blanket. Next to the driver's window, Chief Blunt tapped on the glass.

Babcia rolled down the window a crack. "Can I help you?"

"That was a short trip," Chief Blunt said, her gaze scanning the car.

I squeezed Aunt Coco's arm to keep her from moving. How did Evil Bun know we were hiding in here?

Babcia looked suspiciously at Chief Blunt, but her voice remained calm. "Am I breaking the law?"

"That remains to be seen," Chief Blunt said. "Do you know where Coco Woods is hiding?"

Babcia held a hand up to her ear. "What did you say?"

Chief Blunt repeated her question.

"I'm not hiding anything," Babcia said.

I rolled my eyes under the sweltering blanket. Wasn't the first rule of espionage to say nothing when questioned?

Chief Blunt's gaze shifted to the interior of the vehicle. "How about this...you tell me where she is, and I'll overlook that you're aiding a criminal."

Aunt Coco squeaked. I elbowed my aunt, and she quieted down. Surprisingly, General looked as if he was asleep in my aunt's arms. I thought the dog would be the one to give away our location.

Chief Blunt sidestepped and peered into the backseat. "Did you hear something?"

I held my breath. We were so busted.

Babcia unbuckled her seatbelt and threw open the door, catching Chief Blunt off guard. If she hadn't jumped back, the car door would have hit her.

"Isn't it enough the Gestapo raided my house and took away my guns?" Babcia said, getting up in Chief Blunt's face. "And now you want to lock up my neighbor. What's next? Feed me bread and water? Beat me with a rubber dildo?"

By this time, Babcia was screaming at the top of her lungs, and Chief Blunt backed up to the edge of the driveway. I turned around and peered through the rear window. With the blanket covering my hair and the glare from the afternoon sun, I didn't think Evil Bun saw me. She was too busy trying to get away.

"How often do I have to tell you there are no secret police in Mirror Falls?" Chief Blunt said.

Babcia shook a fist into the air. "That's what Hitler said."

Chief Blunt opened the cruiser's door. "You tell Coco Woods that the longer she runs from the law, the more trouble she is in."

I grinned. Babcia was good. Real good. She pulled out the crazy old lady card and got exactly what she wanted.

Aunt Coco giggled, covering her mouth with her hands. "Another point for Babcia again. Third time this week."

I knew that tone of voice. These two retirees were probably egging each other on, testing the waters to see what they could get away with in town. I should be concerned, but I was more impressed than anything else. They weren't just survivors; they were the Shenanigan Sisters.

After Chief Blunt drove away, Babcia drove her car into the garage. She turned off the engine and rolled down the garage doors. I threw off the smelly blanket and took a deep breath of fresh air. Beggars couldn't be choosers, but where did Babcia get this blanket?

"Babcia, you're a true spymaster," I said.

Babcia looked pleased. "I may be old, but I still have a few tricks up my sleeve."

Aunt Coco got out of the backseat. "Where did you get this blanket? Smells like a dead skunk."

"Not a skunk, but a dead possum," Babcia said. "I took it to Mary's shop. She's stuffing it for me."

"Was it roadkill?" I asked.

Babcia glanced at Aunt Coco. "Yeah. Roadkill. Uh-huh."

Aunt Coco groaned. "Was it the critter eating everything in your garden?"

Babcia shrugged. "Found it dead in my yard. Must have eaten something he wasn't supposed to." She went into the house.

Aunt Coco shook her head, muttering something about Babcia's wild ways. She followed her friend inside, leaving me alone in the garage.

I looked around at the boxes and wondered what was inside each one. Rat poison? I shivered at the thought. Whenever I thought I got things figured out, something else would pop up. Was Babcia a bad influence on my aunt? And did I want to do anything about it?

I would never admit it aloud, but a secret part of me wanted to be a little naughty for a change—to follow Aunt Coco and Babcia's lead. I was so tired of always being the "good girl." I was in my mid-forties with a failed marriage and no career. If my adopted family hadn't abandoned me yet, I probably no longer needed to worry that they would get rid of me. Maybe it was time to let my hair down. Maybe it was time to just be me.

## 11

## SPOOKY STUFF

I stepped into the kitchen. It had cream-colored cabinets and countertops and a navy-blue backsplash. A stainless-steel refrigerator and stove took up an entire wall. A cork bulletin board held notes, items to buy, and coupons. In front of the bay window, overlooking the backyard, was a round table with a lace tablecloth.

The air was heavy with the aroma of potatoes, cheese, cream, and sauerkraut. Babcia had made her special pierogi soup. Yum. I wasn't a big fan of sauerkraut, but the Polish dumplings were the only way to eat this fermented cabbage.

"Good thing I was done fixing lunch when you called, Coco," Babcia said.

I followed Aunt Coco into the living room. The

inside of Babcia's house was painted a neutral tan color. The open floor plan probably provided natural light during the day and a pleasant view of the street in front of the house. Leaning over the sofa, I peered through the window blinds in the living room. The coast was clear. The police cruiser was no longer parked in front of my aunt's house next door.

General greeted Babcia's dachshund, Huntley, by sniffing his butt. The two dogs ran off into the laundry room next to the kitchen.

Aunt Coco took off her top hat, orange wig, and coat, tossing them onto the brown leather sofa. I did the same with the blonde wig and my parka. If only I could remove the itchy wool tights. We returned to the kitchen.

Babcia dished food onto plates on the kitchen island.

"Do you need help with anything?" I asked.

"No, just sit yourself down," Aunt Coco said, opening a bottle of Riesling.

As I watched the two retirees bustling in the kitchen, I realized they probably ate together more often than not. There was an easy rhythm between them as they moved about the kitchen. My anger at my cousins eased a bit. Maybe this was why Aunt

Coco didn't feel an urgent need to finish her kitchen remodel in the last two years. She probably ate better here than by herself at home.

Aunt Coco's cell phone rang, and she answered the call. She held out the phone to me. "It's for you. From your lawyer."

I grabbed the phone and walked into the living room for privacy. I greeted my lawyer and said, "I could use some good news."

The lawyer cleared his throat. "I'm afraid I only have bad news. Your ex-husband's tech company shows zero profits in the last twenty years."

My legs weakened, and I plunked down on the sofa. "How is that possible?"

"That's actually typical for tech companies because of the heavy investment in research and development and the rapid expansion of their market share. And his company filed Chapter 11 three years ago."

"But we had such a lavish lifestyle. There's the big house, the vacations, and the parties."

"And they were all business expenses, contributing to the zero profit."

"But isn't the company worth something? Shouldn't I get half of whatever it is worth?"

"Remember the prenup you signed? The business assets belong to your husband. You only get half of his personal assets, which is about two thousand dollars in a savings account."

"But doesn't he get a salary from the company?"

"His intern has a bigger salary than him. He has used every loophole in the law to keep his income at the poverty level. If he applied for government programs, he'd probably qualify."

I felt sick to my stomach. "What about the new SUV?" Why did I insist my former husband drive the new car? Oh, right. At the time, I didn't think I deserved it.

"It's a company lease, and it's not considered his personal asset. Your ten-year-old pickup truck is a personal asset that can be split, but he said you can keep it."

I cursed my former husband's generosity. "What about retirement accounts? Did he tuck anything away for retirement?"

"He has nothing. Maybe he was counting on your teacher's pension."

Through numb lips, I asked, "Is this decision final? Can I appeal it?"

"It will cost you more time and money. Unless you can prove that he has hidden personal assets, you'll end up in the same place as now."

I thanked my lawyer and hung up. For a long moment, I slumped on the sofa. A part of me knew this outcome was a possibility, but I had secretly hoped my ex-husband was decent enough to see that I wouldn't eat dog food after our divorce. But, unfortunately, I had more faith in him than he deserved.

Aunt Coco came into the living room. She took one look at my face and enveloped me in a warm hug. I blinked away the tears burning in the back of my eyes. I had cried enough tears over my ex-husband this last year, and I would never do it again. My aunt rubbed my back and rocked me back and forth for several long moments.

"I'm fine, Aunt Coco. Let's go have lunch," I said, getting up from the sofa. Even though my voice was thick with emotion, I gave her a wobbly smile.

For the next few minutes, we ate in silence. As the creamy soup and dumplings made their way to my stomach, I felt better. Or maybe it was the second glass of slightly sweet white wine.

I was thankful my aunt and her friend didn't ask about the phone call. They probably guessed the gist of my conversation with my lawyer. It was no secret that I walked away from my marriage with nothing.

"Where are the dogs?" I asked, looking under the table.

"They had lunch and are now napping behind the sofa," Aunt Coco said. "I don't remember the last time General had this much exercise."

"Why is the police cruiser in front of your house, Coco?" Babcia asked. "What did you do this time?"

Aunt Coco topped off our glasses with the last of the Riesling. "I might have left my fingerprints on Fiona's murder weapon."

Babcia's fork clattered onto her plate. "You finally had enough of her harassment. You should've told me what you were doing because I know where you can hide the body."

Aunt Coco shook her head. "It wasn't me."

Babcia nodded. "That's good. Never admit fault."

"This isn't a car accident," I said. "It's serious business."

"We'll have to get you on the road to Canada tonight," Babcia said, ignoring my comment. She probably didn't hear me.

A bubble of mirth rose up, and I started chuckling. Aunt Coco and Babcia turned to smile at me, and soon all three of us were laughing. There was nothing funny about Fiona's death, but it sure was funny that everyone assumed my aunt had something to do with it and was willing to help her escape the authorities. There was a hint of hysteria in my laughter, but if I didn't release the emotion, I would cry.

Eventually, I wiped tears from the corner of my eyes. "Aunt Coco has nothing to do with Fiona's death. She has an alibi."

Babcia held a hand close to her ear. "What?"

I repeated what I said a second time, a little louder.

"You were with Coco and holding down Fiona." Babcia patted my hand. "Good girl. You need to help out your elders. But this means you'll have to leave town, too." She sighed. "I was hoping you'd stay longer this time."

I shook my head. My aunt's friend was undoubtedly filling in the blanks. I must have sat next to her bad ear. I repeated myself a third time, yelling. I was surprised I didn't wake the dogs. Babcia must have worn them out with exercise. Or maybe they were used to raised voices in this house.

Babcia blinked. "Oh. That's no fun."

I took a gulp of wine. I couldn't believe my aunt's friend was disappointed that we weren't Fiona's killers.

"That's not the important part." Aunt Coco threw her napkin onto the table. "If we continue with this mission, we'll need equipment. Something that will give us an advantage over Everly."

Babcia leaned forward in her chair. "I can't help you there. The Gestapo raided my house and took away my guns."

I blinked. Who exactly was the secret police, and why did Babcia have more than one gun? At her age and with her cataracts, she didn't need to own any weapons. It was bad enough that she was still driving.

My aunt and her friend exchanged a look. I sighed inwardly. I had seen that guilty look enough times among my former students to know something had happened. I wasn't even going to ask and derail this conversation.

"What kind of equipment are we talking about here? Walkie talkies?" I asked. "Night vision goggles?"

Aunt Coco shrugged. "We'll dig through your uncle's foot locker. There might be something there we can use. He had brought home souvenirs from his missions."

I got up from the table and almost slid sideways. Actually, all three of us weren't too steady on our feet. "I think we should follow the dogs' lead and nap. We can go next door after we wake up."

Aunt Coco and Babcia agreed with me. They disappeared into the bedrooms, and I crashed onto the sofa in the living room. As soon as my head hit the cushion, it was lights out.

A little while later, I woke to a wet tongue licking my nose and inhaling someone else's bad breath. My eyes popped open, and General grinned at me. Oh, joy. Doggy breath. I sat up on the sofa and studied my aunt's new pet.

I thought corgis were barkers who didn't do well with strangers. But this dog was socialized and didn't appear to have separation anxiety.

"Are you my Uncle Gabriel? Bark once for yes, and two for no," I said.

I felt silly, but there was no one around. And after the events of the last two days, a little silliness would lighten the mood.

The dog woofed as if he understood me.

The dog had to be answering my tone of voice rather than my actual question. Maybe I should try again with a harder question.

"Are you a girl dog?" I asked.

Woof. Woof.

I blinked. The corgi had answered no like he knew he was a male dog. He was doing a good job of pretending to answer my questions. Maybe my aunt had been training him. After all, corgis were intelligent animals.

"Am I a girl?" I asked.

General's brown eyes rolled toward the ceiling. Woof.

Now, this was starting to get weird. I glanced around the living room but didn't see anything that could prompt the dog to answer my questions correctly. Not that I was expecting anything to be here.

Goose flesh peppered my skin, and the hair on the back of my neck stiffened. General bumped his head against my hand as if to comfort me.

"Are you my Uncle Gabriel?" I was glad there was no one listening in on this conversation. How could someone feel both silly and terrified at the same time?

Woof.

"Do you have unfinished business?"

Woof.

"Is it my aunt?"

Woof. Woof.

"Is it the house remodel?"

Woof. Woof.

Most Asian cultures believe in reincarnation in one form or another. So it wasn't surprising Aunt

Coco believed in it. And now I wasn't sure what to think.

However, from the little I knew about Buddhism, for my uncle to be reincarnated as an animal meant he was going backward on the karma wheel. Uncle Gabriel was a good person, a pillar of the community. As a three-star general, he probably had had to make some tough calls, but he didn't take his responsibility lightly. Thus, it would be impossible for my uncle to be reincarnated at a lower level than a human.

Next, my uncle was a Christian. So, my aunt's belief in reincarnation probably didn't apply to this situation. If there was a link between General and my uncle, then my uncle might have sent the corgi to keep my aunt company like a guardian angel.

Whatever the case, the fact that the dog had shown up on my uncle's death anniversary was a little spooky. And this silent communication between my aunt and her pet wasn't something I had ever witnessed. Maybe Aunt Coco made things up like her neighbor, and the dog was an excuse to put forth outrageous ideas she wouldn't normally say out loud. Yes, I was more comfortable with this idea.

I rubbed my temples. I should have passed on the second glass of wine. No, there was no spooky business here. General was only answering my tone rather than my questions.

Aunt Coco strolled into the living room, clapping her hands. "Time to get up and look through your uncle's footlocker. We need to find some weapons of mass destruction."

I peeked through the living room window blinds. A police cruiser was parked in front of Aunt Coco's house again. With dusk approaching and no streetlights, I couldn't tell if the driver was Evil Bun or another officer. I wondered if the white cargo van was still parked next to the alley. In either case, we couldn't go boldly out the front door and make our way into Aunt Coco's house. We would have to sneak in like thieves.

## 12

# THREE GOLDILOCKS

As I crept after my aunt and her friend across the dark yards connecting their two properties, I regretted the second glass of wine. It was obvious from our conversation that I was the only responsible adult here, and I had let these two retirees ply me with alcohol so I would do their bidding. Shame on me.

First, we could have waited until the next morning to look through Uncle Gabriel's footlocker. Moving around in the semi-darkness with two elderly women was a horrible idea. What if one of them fell? It would be poetic justice if my Aunt Coco broke her hip, but I would feel horrible rather than satisfied.

Second, the police cruiser was still parked up front. At this point, I wondered if the officer had fallen asleep. But what if this person thought we were thieves breaking into Aunt Coco's house? I would hate to get shot by accident.

Third, it was almost dinnertime. Aunt Coco wasn't someone who could miss a meal. The special combination of hunger and anger came out in tantrums that could be worse than a toddler.

Once we got in from the back door, we turned on the flashlight app on our cell phones. We couldn't risk turning on the lights. As we crept up the creaking stairs, tension settled on my neck and shoulders. Our cell phones lit the hallway, casting creepy shadows. We moved cautiously to avoid falling or making noises.

Aunt Coco and Babcia were smart enough to press up against the wall, as I pulled down the stairs for the attic in the upstairs hallway. A layer of dust rained down on me. As I climbed the stairs to the attic, my nose wrinkled at the musty scent of old wood and stale air.

The darkness was all-consuming, and I could barely make out the shapes of the old wooden beams that crisscrossed above our heads. The dirty windows glowed in the darkness, but the light was too faint to be of any use. The cold was intense, and I started to shiver despite my thick parka. The attic was finished in that the drywall hid the wood framing. However, it was still one cavernous space used for decades as storage.

We searched the attic carefully, moving slowly to avoid the boxes and old furniture left behind by previous owners. The beams of our lights danced around the room, illuminating corners and crevices. As we moved deeper into the attic, I couldn't shake the feeling that we were being watched. The feeling of dread and unease continued to grow, and I found myself glancing over my shoulder every few seconds.

"Now, where is the footlocker?" Aunt Coco mumbled to herself. She seemed unaffected by the cavernous dark attic.

Eventually, we found it tucked away behind a dresser and covered in a thick layer of dust. Aunt Coco and Babcia carefully lifted the lid. Inside, we found a cache of weapons—grenades, rifles, handguns, crossbows, slingshots, knives, and daggers. In addition, there were night vision goggles, binoculars, ham radios, and even walkie talkies. Tickle me pink. We had hit the mother lode.

My heart started to race. Was it even legal for us to own half of this stuff? What would happen if Chief Blunt found us with these weapons?

Aunt Coco and Babcia were already handling the items with excitement, examining each one with a critical eye.

*Bang!*

I jumped at the sound and dropped my cell phone. The beam from the flashlight app spun around the attic like a disco ball.

"Did you hear that?" Aunt Coco asked, looking around in confusion.

"What?" Babcia said, holding up a hand to her ear.

"Police!" someone called from inside the house. The lights came on downstairs and lit up the opening for the attic. Footsteps pounded on the stairs.

"Close the footlocker," I said, grabbing one corner of the lid.

Aunt Coco grabbed the other corner of the lid, and we hefted it into place.

"We have to go downstairs and keep the cops away from the attic," I said, leading the way with my hands up in the air.

"Police!" the voice called out again, louder and closer this time.

As we descended the stairs, I called out, "We are the homeowners."

When we reached the bottom of the stairs, Chief Blunt and two other officers were waiting for us, guns drawn and pointed at us.

"Hands up! Get down on the ground!" one of the officers shouted.

I raised my hands and got down on the ground as instructed.

Aunt Coco placed both hands on her hips. "Everly, what the waffle? Did you break my front door?"

Chief Blunt's head swiveled to stare at my aunt. "How did you get in here? I had someone watching the house."

"I know," Aunt Coco said.

"What are you doing in the dark?" Chief Blunt said.

"It's my house," Aunt Coco said. "I can do whatever I want. You're lucky I still have my bra on."

One of the officers' faces reddened. I wanted to laugh at his reaction, but I didn't think it would help the situation.

"Your neighbor across the street said there was a burglary in progress," Chief Blunt said.

"That man jumps at his own shadow," Aunt Coco said.

"Your neighbor said there were flashlight beams like several people were searching the house," Chief Blunt said.

I looked around, and since it didn't seem like we would get shot by accident, I got up from the floor. "Thank you for your timely response, but we don't need your services. You can leave now."

Everyone ignored me.

"Why didn't you turn on the lights?" one of the officers asked.

"We were trying to catch the ghost who lives in the attic." Aunt Coco said this with such a straight face even I believed her.

"I told you she's a nut," one of the officers mumbled to his partner.

"Coco Woods, we need you to come down to the station," Chief Blunt said.

"You can't come into someone's home and take them in for questioning," Babcia said. "This is the United States of America. You can't do this here. Who do you think you are? The secret police?"

Chief Blunt sighed and rubbed a hand over her

face. A small part of me felt sorry for her. The dark eye bags and wrinkles on her uniform showed that she didn't have a restful night—if she even got any sleep. "We have been looking for Coco all day. We found her prints on the murder weapon."

"How do you know they are my aunt's prints?" I asked.

Chief Blunt swiveled her gaze at me. "This wouldn't be the first time I've taken her down to the station. We have her prints on file, and they are a match."

"Are you going to take a mug shot this time?" Aunt Coco asked.

My aunt didn't look the least bit concerned, and this scared me.

"Wait a minute," I said, making the time-out sign with my hands. "Do you have a warrant for this arrest?"

"I am asking for Coco's cooperation," Chief Blunt said. "If she's innocent, she has nothing to worry about."

"Aunt Coco, you should call your lawyer first," I said.

Chief Blunt glared at me. "Perry has probably gone home for the day."

Evil Bun being on a first-name basis with my

aunt's lawyer was terrifying. What had my aunt been doing this last year when I took my eyes off the ball to deal with my divorce?

I glanced at my watch. It was already six o'clock. The law office probably didn't open until nine the next morning.

"There's no point in bringing Aunt Coco in this evening," I said. "She won't say a word until her lawyer gets there."

I gave my aunt a pointed look. Aunt Coco zipped her lips to let me know she got my message.

"She will show up tomorrow morning with her lawyer," I said.

"How do I know you won't drive up to Canada?" Chief Blunt said.

Aunt Coco held up a palm like she was being sworn in. "I promise not to run away. Pinkie swear."

Chief Blunt shook her handcuffs in front of my aunt. "Photo op."

Aunt Coco thrust her cell phone into my hands. "You know the code to unlock it. Use this while I'm in the slammer." She turned to Chief Blunt. "I'm ready to be handcuffed. Cedar, snap a photo. Everly, make sure you're standing next to me. The rest of you boys, come crowd around me."

The officers glanced at Chief Blunt and followed my aunt's direction.

The corner of Evil Bun's lips curled and straightened. She was both amused and annoyed at the same time. Maybe this was a good thing. It meant she didn't have any ill will toward my aunt.

"If you want to take that picture, make it quick," Chief Blunt said. "But I am not posing."

Aunt Coco smiled and made peace signs with her fingers.

"Are you for real, Aunt Coco?" I said. "You're willing to give away your freedom for photos?"

Aunt Coco turned to Babcia. "Make it quick."

Babcia snapped several photos with her cell phone.

A few minutes later, the officers got into their vehicles and drove off. My aunt got into the back of Chief Blunt's cruiser, and Babcia started to climb in after her.

"Babcia, what are you doing?" Chief Blunt asked.

Babcia held a hand up to her ear. "What?"

Chief Blunt shifted until she was speaking directly into Babcia's other ear. "I said, what are you doing?"

"What do you think?" Babcia said. "I'm keeping an eye on you. Making sure you're following procedure and ensuring my best friend doesn't disappear into a black hole."

"But why are you in the back of my car?" Chief Blunt asked.

Babcia raised an eyebrow. "Do you want me on the road in the dark with my cataracts? You might as well just give me a lift to the station." She held up a hand as if she was being sworn in. "I promise I will not kick the back of your seat. Pinkie swear."

Chief Blunt glanced at me. "Can't you give her a ride to the station?"

I held up both hands, palms out. "I don't have GPS in my old truck." And I wasn't going to make it easy on Evil Bun to take my aunt away.

Chief Blunt sighed and closed the rear door of the cruiser.

As I watched Evil Bun drive away, I had never felt so terrified in my life. Not even when I found out I had no money at the beginning of my divorce. After all, I had friends in town, and I figured if I kept going through my contacts list, someone would eventually lend a hand.

While I was in my hometown, it was still a strange place. I hadn't called this place home in over three decades. Not since my parents' death. My brother wasn't in town, and I knew less than a handful of people but didn't know them well enough to ask them for help.

My chest felt tight, and my breaths became shallow. As my body grew hot and flush, I started sweating like I just had a workout, but without the happy hormones. What do I do? Who should I call?

Something bumped my leg, and I jumped. It was General. Somehow, he had gotten out of Babcia's house and now rubbed against my ankle like a cat. This was so unexpected that it snapped me out of a panic attack. I bent down and hugged General, and the tightness in my chest loosened.

As I stared into the corgi's warm, brown eyes, I took several deep breaths. I still didn't believe he was my Uncle Gabriel, but there was something to be said for having an animal friend.

First, I wasn't alone. I had Aunt Coco's cell phone. This gave me access to all her friends, which wasn't an insignificant number. If needed, I could call in the cavalry—literally, because I'm sure she was on a first-name basis with other generals and officers from the military.

Second, I could call Josh. He could be on the plane and home within a day. This would be a last resort. Even if Aunt Coco got charged with Fiona's murder, it would take a while to go through the process. The law didn't work at the speed of light.

Third, there was Babcia. With her cantankerous friend bird dogging things at the police station, Aunt Coco wasn't alone. I had time to figure out my next move.

## 13

## BOSS OF ME

My stomach rumbled. It looked like my next move was dinner. General bumped my leg, trying to herd me. All right. He also knew I needed food.

I marched to Babcia's house, let myself in through the side gate, and went into the kitchen from the unlocked back door with General dogging my steps.

Huntley ran over, wagging his tail, but stopped in his tracks when he didn't see Babcia behind me. He ran outside the door, circled the yard, and came back, looking for his owner.

I scratched his ears. "Sorry, boy. It looks like we got Babcia mixed up in this murder business."

As I heated up the leftover dumpling soup on the

stovetop, I scrolled through my aunt's cell phone contacts, looking for a Perry since I didn't know the lawyer's last name. Eventually, I found a Perry Goodwin and left a message about what happened to my aunt. I asked him to call me back at my aunt's phone number.

I fed the dogs, and I forced myself to eat. I didn't have much of an appetite, but I had to keep my strength up. After the dumpling soup, I chased it down with a pint of ice cream. I was stress eating again, but I couldn't help myself. I clipped the leashes on the dogs, and the three of us set off for a walk, so I could mull things over.

Duncan was the obvious suspect because Fiona's death gave him access to his nephew's trust fund. Didn't people often kill for either money or love? Even Fiona's baker thought Duncan was a likely suspect. However, he only disappeared for a few minutes while we were gathered around the lumber pile. Was that enough time to grab the hammer from two doors down, take out his aunt, and run back to smear a bloody fingerprint on the tea shop's door? Maybe, but very unlikely.

After we sorted things out with the lawyer tomorrow, I needed to pay a visit to Juan Perez, Fiona's widower. Duncan claimed Juan had the most to gain from Fiona's death—his freedom. By all accounts, he was a long-suffering husband who had put up with his wife's infidelity. And he couldn't divorce her because of her connection to Malcolm Spencer, the town's informal godfather.

If all this were true, wouldn't Juan be worse off with Fiona's death? Surely, Malcolm would want payback for his daughter's murder. And this would put Juan squarely in Malcolm's crosshairs.

As we passed the back-alley entrance, I didn't see the white cargo van. My aunt was right. It was just a parked vehicle, and I made a molehill out of nothing. The dogs did their business, and I bent down to retrieve their little gifts with the plastic bags looped around the leash handle. General and Huntley gave me their goofy little smiles, clearly secure in the knowledge that they were the boss of me.

When we rounded the corner of the block, I stopped dead in my tracks. The white cargo van was parked in front of my aunt's house. The person inside must have moved the vehicle when the police cruisers approached the neighborhood. And now this person was back.

I squared my shoulders and resumed walking. The person in the van probably wasn't on the lookout for me. And as long as I didn't approach

Aunt Coco's house, I was just another neighbor walking her dogs. Once inside Babcia's house, I locked up and turned off the living room lights. I peered at the van from behind the blinds of the living room window, wishing for my uncle's night vision goggles. But I wasn't desperate enough to make another trek across the dark yards to retrieve them from the attic.

When it was finally bedtime, I made a show of checking all the windows and doors. I dragged the doggie beds from the bedrooms to the living room. I didn't want the dogs to get lonely without their owners. Okay, who was I kidding? I was afraid to sleep alone in the living room. After I made myself a comfortable nest on the sofa with the blanket and pillow from the hall closet, I turned off all the lights in the house. With General on my lap, I sat on the sofa, staring through the window blinds at the white cargo van. I didn't sleep for a very long time.

WHEN MY AUNT'S cell phone alarm rang the next morning, I woke up in the guest bedroom with General by my side. As I rubbed my eyes, I sat up in bed. It took a couple of seconds to orient myself, and

I grabbed my glasses to bring the room into focus. The last thing I remembered was staring at the white cargo van from the living room sofa. After that, I had no recollection of coming into Babcia's guest bedroom.

I made the bed and went into the hallway bathroom to take care of my morning business. I didn't recognize the person in the mirror. Eye bags. Wild hair—not the up-all-night escapade hair—more of a witchy hag hair. And where did the gray roots come from? Didn't I touch up my hair...had it been weeks?

When I stumbled into the living room, I froze in my tracks. The blanket on the sofa was thrown on the carpet like someone had gotten up in the middle of the night. And that someone was me. Shut the door. I was sleepwalking again.

As I put the blanket and pillow away, my hands shook. I'd started sleepwalking as a child shortly after my parents' deaths, but eventually, it went away. There were some scary moments when I would walk out of the house in the middle of the night, but luckily, someone was always awake at a military base. Why did the sleepwalking come back? Why wasn't it an issue during the divorce?

I sighed—nothing I could do about it at the moment. I needed to focus on the things that needed my attention. I filled the food bowls and changed the water for the dogs. I opened the pet door so that they could take care of their business in the backyard.

As the coffee maker worked its magic and filled a mug, I called my aunt's lawyer, Perry Goodwin. It was still too early, but he picked up right away.

"Coco," Perry said on the phone, "I thought we agreed that you wouldn't need my services for the rest of the month. If you keep calling me like this, I'll think you want to spend more time with me."

My eyes widened. Ooh-la-la. First, Malcolm Spencer, and now, Perry Goodwin. When did my aunt become so popular with the men in town?

"Hi, Mr. Goodwin," I said. "This is Cedar Woods, Coco's niece. Unfortunately, my aunt is in trouble again." I explained the situation.

"First, you can call me Perry," the lawyer said. "Second, I mostly handle civil cases and never worked on a murder case before."

"Can you recommend anyone?" I asked.

"There's only five of us in town, and we mostly handle civil cases," Perry said. "You can probably find a criminal lawyer in a bigger town. I can go down to the station and see what I can do. However, if we have to go to trial, I recommend you get someone who specializes in that area."

"This will not go to trial. Someone set up my aunt."

Perry sighed. "That's what Coco always says. I need to talk to my secretary so she can rearrange my schedule."

I thanked the lawyer profusely, glad to have someone competent on our side. We agreed to meet at the station in half an hour.

In San Jose, I had to twist into a pretzel to fit in. But everyone accepted me here as if I automatically had credibility in the community. It was a nice feeling.

General padded back into the kitchen and put his paws on my lap. As I sipped the coffee, I patted his head. First things first. Before I duke it out with Evil Bun, I needed to put on my battle armor.

"Be good, buddy," I said to General. "I'm off to rescue Aunt Coco."

I took the mug with me as I trekked across the yards toward my aunt's house. With all the people watching the house, I was too jumpy to use the front door. So instead, I let myself in through the back door and hurried upstairs to the bathroom.

I spent the next fifteen minutes putting on my contacts and makeup. Luckily, I still had half a closet full of designer clothes—the other half had been sold off to support my current lifestyle of sweatpants and T-shirts.

But I understood the subtle power shift that came with presenting a polished appearance. I put on my "power" pantsuit, a regal violet suit by Emilia Wickstead. It was three years old, but I didn't think anyone in town would notice. I held onto the black suede pumps and a black leather Saint Laurent purse (my only designer purse left) in one hand and the empty coffee mug in the other. I was ready to do battle with Evil Bun.

From the upstairs bedroom window, I didn't see the white cargo van in front of the house. Good. I didn't want the van driver to associate me with my aunt's house. I strolled downstairs and into the kitchen to place the dirty coffee mug in the sink. I didn't think Babcia would mind that I return the mug to her later.

In the drying rack next to the kitchen sink were the mugs Aunt Coco and I had used yesterday. When Evil Bun had knocked, we ran out of the house through the back door. Neither one of us had time to wash the mugs. Had my aunt's cleaning person been here?

As I stared at the fine china, gooseflesh peppered my skin. The house groaned and creaked, the floorboards and ceiling protesting every move of the wind. I ran to the back door, put on my shoes, and power walked to the garage behind the house. I didn't know why, but I was afraid to be alone.

When I pulled out of the back alley, I glanced up and down the street. No white cargo van. Nice. The tension left my shoulders, and I drove the rest of the way in a more relaxed state of mind. I had learned to roll with the punches from my Uncle Gabriel, but this didn't mean I didn't worry from time to time. Who was I kidding? I hadn't stopped worrying since my brother called and asked me to come home.

The police station was a former train station, a small white clapboard building hastily put up when Mirror Falls was still a logging town and the railroad transported lumber. The trains were long gone, and the rails were covered with concrete. The original wood shingle roof was now a gray composite. Someone had planted pine trees around the building—probably so it would look less stark—and the air was thick with the smell of pine and wet earth. The only positive thing I could say about the police station was that it was functional.

The inside was one open floor plan with partitions to divide the space. An elderly man sat reading a thriller novel at the L-shaped counter in the reception area. His name tag with large print said he was called Marshall and a volunteer. The three plastic chairs against the wall in front of the counter were empty. The air was filled with the pungent aroma of stale coffee—probably from the pot in the far wall—and the reek of old cigarette smoke that had seeped into the walls and flooring. Even the HVAC system couldn't get rid of decades of smoking in the building.

The two desks on the other side of the counter were unoccupied. The police force consisted of the chief and two officers. It made sense the officers were out patrolling the neighborhoods. But where were Chief Blunt and Aunt Coco?

As I walked up to the L-shaped counter, butterflies fluttered in my stomach.

Before I could speak, Marshall greeted me. "You must be Coco's niece. You look just like her."

I didn't bother to correct him. While Aunt Coco and I were not blood related, we were both Chinese. Growing up, I was often mistaken for her daughter, which had irritated my mom and amused my aunt.

Marshall was probably in his seventies. He made up for his bald head with bushy white eyebrows and an even bushier mustache. It looked as if he had three dead caterpillars on his weathered face.

"Yes, I am Cedar Woods. Can I see my aunt?" I said.

Marshall got up from his chair. "It's 'bout time you got here. Everly is at the courthouse getting the warrant for your aunt's arrest. Coco will be charged for Fiona's murder."

## 14

### CARNIVAL FUN HOUSE

I gripped the countertop, my knuckles turning white. Everything was happening too fast. It felt like a dream, an awful nightmare. Were fingerprints on the murder weapon enough to charge Aunt Coco with murder?

Someone patted my hand, and I glanced up into Marshall's concerned eyes.

"Are you okay, my dear?" Marshall asked. From the slow, deliberate way he formed the words, it was clear that this wasn't the first time he had asked this question.

"No, I am not okay," I said, surprising myself with the raw honesty in my voice. "I am not okay."

But I had always been okay before. I had always managed to figure things out. How was it different this time? A murder seemed too big for someone like me to figure out. If the trained professionals couldn't figure it out, how was I—an unemployed divorcee— supposed to figure it out?

I blinked, trying to process my thoughts. What did my employment or marital status have to do with this? Was I looking for an excuse to hold myself back? To play it small because I was afraid...of success?

A man in a suit came out of the room on the left, distracting me from further thoughts. This wasn't the time to freak out.

"Cedar Woods?" the man called out.

I nodded. "Yes?"

The man walked over and held out his hand. "Perry Goodwin."

Perry was about my age. He was tall but beanpole thin. His hair was graying at the temples, giving him a distinguished look. His eyes were a pale green, almost hazel, under the fluorescent light. The lawyer wore a dark blue suit, and a wedding band glinted on his finger. Now, why did he flirt over the phone when he thought Aunt Coco had called him?

"Marshall said Aunt Coco will be charged with Fiona's murder," I said. My voice wobbled, and I took a deep breath. If I started crying now, I might never stop.

"I will do everything possible to get Coco out on bail," Perry said.

"Can I see my aunt?" I asked.

Perry shook his head. "The officers are out, and Chief Blunt is at the courthouse. Marshall is not authorized to let you see Coco."

I still wanted to see Aunt Coco, but I had to be patient. "Have you seen her?"

"Coco is fine, just cranky because she didn't get any sleep last night," Perry said. "She was in the same holding cell as Sally the Drunk, who was singing all night."

"Did she get any food?" I asked.

Marshall nodded. "But she refused it. Said she was on a hunger strike."

I was relieved at my aunt's sassy response. This meant my aunt was still in good spirits.

"The police released the tea shop and coffee shop," Perry said. "They have gotten what they needed."

"I thought they didn't have the staff to process everything so quickly," I said.

Perry shrugged. "Overtime? I don't know."

"Where is Babcia?" I asked.

"She's trailing after Chief Blunt, the poor woman."

Having Babcia dog your steps was a trial I would not wish on my enemy. "Thank you for your help," I said. "But what should I do now?"

"Why don't you do something to take your mind off of all this?" Perry said. "Take in a movie, or go for a walk. Anything to keep your mind occupied. I will call you as soon as I have more news."

I knew he was right. Distracting myself was the best thing I could do right now. And the best distraction would be to find the real murderer. My aunt wasn't spending her golden years in jail because I made the stupid decision to pick up a hammer.

No, picking up the hammer wasn't stupid. I didn't know what was going on. A woman had to be able to defend herself. It was just pure bad luck the murderer grabbed the hammer and set up my aunt as the fall guy.

A few minutes later, I drove the few blocks back to Old Town. I could have walked, but my feet were sore from all the exercise yesterday, and I didn't want to mess up my only pair of designer heels.

I parked in front of the tea shop. The pile of lumber was gone, along with the crime scene tapes. But, amazingly, the front door of Fiona's coffee shop was wide open. Did someone open the shop for business?

My stomach rumbled. I only had coffee for breakfast this morning and could use a pastry. I glanced at Fiona's coffee shop again. From all accounts, the baker was the coffee shop's only saving grace. If nothing else, I should talk to whoever was running the shop and see if I could get additional leads.

As I trotted up the boardwalk steps, Luke's truck pulled up behind mine. His shiny F-150 was newer and had more hauling and towing capacity than my old truck. Luckily, I didn't measure my worth by the size of my vehicle.

My heart skipped a beat at the sight of Luke. He wore loose-fitting tan cargo pants, a long-sleeved white shirt, and a blue down parka. I was a little disappointed he wasn't in his lumberjack outfit.

I was surprised by my sudden attraction toward him. It was probably the stress of the murder investigation. I felt like a fish out of water and definitely out of my depth, but he was a family friend and an ally I could rely on, even if it appeared that he didn't like me very much.

Luke caught up to me on the boardwalk. His gaze

swept me from head to toe. "Are you running for mayor or something?"

It took me a moment to figure out what he was referring to—my power suit. "I was hoping to intimidate Chief Blunt."

The corner of his mouth twitched, but he gave me a deadpan expression. "Did it work?"

"I didn't even see her," I said.

Luke chuckled. "Not much intimidates Everly."

I gave him a sideways glance. Just how well did he know Evil Bun? I gave myself a mental shake. Why did I care? "What are you doing here?"

"Babcia said Coco is being charged for Fiona's murder and that you are still in the area. So, I figured I'd look around." Luke gestured at the coffee shop. "Why don't we start there?"

We approached the entrance—it was propped open. Inside was surprisingly clean and orderly—far more than when I had last visited. We were met by a young Hispanic woman with her brown hair pulled into a ponytail and thick glasses perched on her button nose. She wore a sweatshirt and jeans and held a rag in her hands.

"*Sí?*" the woman asked.

Luke stepped forward and spoke to her in Spanish. I was impressed.

The cleaning woman smiled, looked at me, and then back at Luke. Then she nodded and gestured us towards the kitchen door with a tilt of her head.

"What did you say?" I asked.

"I told her we were looking for the person in charge of the coffee shop," Luke said.

As we stepped through the doorway, I braced myself. Surely, someone had cleaned up the crime scene, or the cleaning lady wouldn't be so calm about letting us through. When I saw Chrissy Lane emerge from the walk-in pantry holding a clipboard, I let go of the breath I didn't even know I was holding. No dead body. No blood.

The tile floor had been scrubbed to a shine, and the countertops and tables were wiped down. The stainless steel appliances glinted under the fluorescent light, and the bleach smell lingered in the air. The kitchen was much cleaner than I had expected. It was almost to the point of being sterile—not a single piece of blood or clue remained. I didn't know if Chrissy's baking was any good, but she certainly was efficient at cleaning up.

Chrissy still looked tired and pale like she hadn't gotten over her illness. Even though she smiled warmly, she was surprised by our sudden appearance in the kitchen. "Oh! Hi, there. We are not open for customers today."

. "How did you get this all cleaned up so quickly?" I said, waving my hands to indicate the kitchen. "My aunt's shop still has fingerprint dust over everything." Actually, I wasn't sure what was the condition of my aunt's shop, but Chrissy didn't know this. And I wasn't lying because there probably was dust everywhere.

Chrissy looked away, embarrassed. "This is Malcolm Spencer's doing," she admitted softly, not meeting my eyes as she spoke. "He's good at cleaning up messes...like this one."

The fine hair on the back of my neck stiffened. I'd heard enough about Malcolm Spencer in the last few days to know that I should be wary. What had he dug up about Fiona's murder? He had more resources than I did, and if he was truly sweet on Aunt Coco, maybe he could be a potential ally. I shivered at the thought. If I had to make a deal with the devil to free my aunt, I would do it.

"How are you feeling? Have you gotten over your illness yet?" I asked.

"Thank you for asking, but my problems are nothing compared to everything else. It's been hard since Fiona died so suddenly," Chrissy said, her voice breaking. She took a deep breath. "She was like my sister."

We shared an awkward silence for what felt like an eternity before I finally spoke up again, asking the question that had been on my mind since we entered the kitchen. "Besides Duncan Spencer, who else would want to kill Fiona?"

Chrissy wrinkled her nose as if she had smelled something unpleasant. "Why are you questioning me?"

I tried to appear nonchalant, but my heart was racing. "My aunt is being charged for Fiona's murder."

Chrissy's eyes widened, and her hand flew to cover her mouth. "Not Coco." She shook her head. "I don't believe this."

I saw Luke snooping around the kitchen from the corner of my eye. He opened and closed the cupboards quietly. I returned my focus to Chrissy, hoping to keep her distracted so Luke could continue his search.

"I don't think Chief Blunt will do anything to exonerate my aunt," I said. "It's up to me to look into Fiona's murder."

I didn't mean to announce this, but it was time to turn up the heat. The murderer had to be someone from the community. This wasn't a random act of violence. This was someone who knew Aunt Coco and Fiona's ongoing feud. If this person thought they were home free because the police had arrested someone, then I wasn't going to let them rest easy.

"Are you sure that's wise?" Chrissy looked at me with concern. "Maybe you should leave this to the professionals."

"And the professional is busy charging my aunt," I said. "Even though I didn't know or like Fiona Spencer, someone needs to make sure her killer didn't get away with murder. She didn't deserve to die just because she was an unpleasant person."

Chrissy gave me a hesitant nod as if she understood my point even though she didn't agree with me. "How can I help?"

"I need information," I said, not wanting to beat around the bush any longer. "Any names or leads."

"Well...there's Duncan..." Chrissy's voice trailed off.

I shook my head. "I've already spoken to him, and he's not the killer."

Chrissy frowned. "But he'll have access to all the money..."

"Duncan has an alibi," I said.

Chrissy opened her mouth to speak but then

decided against it. Instead, she glanced at the clock on the wall next to the refrigerator. "I'm sorry, but I need to finish cleaning the place and putting together the inventory for the shop."

"Who's asking you to do this? I thought you were the baker."

"Baker and assistant. Duncan asked me to fill in as temporary manager until the family figures things out."

It looked like Duncan wasn't the only one who had gained financially from Fiona's death. However, I didn't think Chrissy would murder her friend and employer for the possibility of promotion. For all she knew, someone else could have stepped in as manager.

A door slammed shut. I glanced around.

"Where did Luke go?" Chrissy asked.

We both glanced at the back door that led out to the back alley.

"Smoking break?" I said. Should I keep talking to Chrissy to keep her from looking for Luke?

"Luke isn't a smoker." Chrissy ran to the back door, opened it, and popped her head out. "Luke?"

No answer.

I trotted after her. "What is it?"

"Why did he leave so suddenly?" Chrissy asked.

I couldn't tell Chrissy that Luke had probably found something. "We are expecting a call from Perry Goodwin. Maybe he left to talk to the lawyer in private."

Chrissy frowned. "But shouldn't your aunt's lawyer call you?"

I didn't want to lie outright, but she had a point. "My phone doesn't get reception sometimes. I better get going. If that call is from Perry, it's important. We need to post bail for my aunt."

As I made my way back to the tea shop, I wondered what Luke had found that made him bolt from the coffee shop. Hopefully, it was something overlooked by the police rather than a diarrhea attack.

# 15

## CAT NINJA

Luke's truck was still parked behind mine, so he was still in the area. I unlocked the front door of the tea shop and left it propped open. Hopefully, Luke would come in once the coast was clear. I was burning with curiosity, but I didn't want to call him and have his ringing cell phone give away his location.

Dust whirled in the pale sunlight coming in from the shop windows. The contractor had removed his tools, leaving behind a screwdriver, a measuring tape, and boxes of building materials. A faint noise came from the back, giving me a sense of déjà vu.

My heart pounded against my chest. What if the killer came back to plant more evidence? That made no sense. The police were in the process of charging my aunt for Fiona's murder. Why take the risk?

"Luke? Is that you?" I called out. My voice was shriller than normal, making me sound like I sucked in helium. If this wasn't a sign I wasn't meant to be a superhero, then I didn't know what other sign I needed.

"I'm in the kitchen," Luke called out.

With a sigh of relief, I strolled into the kitchen and squinted at the glare of the overhead fluorescent light against the stainless-steel appliances. Unlike the front room, the kitchen had narrow windows at the top of the far wall, which only let the occupants see if it was day or night. I made a mental note to talk to the contractor about adjusting the lighting.

Luke stood at the island with the contents of a black purse lined up neatly on the countertop. He had on a pair of clear plastic gloves, the kind used in food preparation. He must have gotten the gloves from the coffee shop when he was snooping around in the kitchen.

"Whose bag is that?" I asked.

"Fiona's," Luke said.

My eyes widened. "You stole Fiona's purse?"

Luke picked up a bundle of folded paper. "Borrowed."

I didn't want to argue semantics with him, especially when done was done. "How did you get in here?"

"Back door. Key."

I shifted my gaze to the island countertop. Even though I couldn't see the label on the purse, the soft leather had a luxurious shine like it had been buffed to a high sheen. The brass zippers were shiny with no noticeable scratches or tarnish. There was a compact mirror, a tube of lipstick, a red leather wallet, a set of keys, and a cell phone. Each item was arranged in a neat line like a child might line up his plastic army soldiers. I wondered if Luke arranged his own things like this.

As I stood there, looking at Fiona's things, I felt a moment of sadness. Even though I didn't know Fiona—and the part I had seen, I didn't like—she was still once alive with her own set of joys and struggles. It wasn't right that someone murdered her. This person needed to serve time for the crime.

I never before felt the desire to right the injustices of this world. My late uncle and my cousins were the heroes who took on this role so the rest of us could have regular lives. I wasn't cut out to be a hero, but at this moment, I had to step up to the plate. I couldn't bury my head in the sand on this one. I was afraid, but what choice did I have?

"Where did you find Fiona's purse? How did the police miss it?" I asked.

"It was inside the walk-in pantry, behind a bag of coffee beans," Luke said. "That's an odd place to put a purse."

"Maybe Fiona didn't put it there." If the police had done a proper job of investigating the crime scene, they would have found the purse. Why didn't Chief Blunt look for Fiona's purse in the first place? Almost every woman I knew carried one.

Luke spread the bundle of paper out and tapped on it. "Look at this. Divorce papers."

I studied the papers. Fiona had filled in the forms to dissolve her marriage, but had it been served? My gaze moved across the documents. No signature. "Who else knew Fiona was seeking a divorce?" I muttered to myself.

This blew Duncan's theory out of the water. He said Juan would kill Fiona to get his freedom, but his freedom was right here. Fiona wanted out, and she had started the process before her death. But the papers hadn't been served. Maybe Juan didn't know.

I turned to Luke. "Who was Fiona having an affair with?"

Luke shrugged. "I have no idea. It was common knowledge that she was cheating on her husband."

"Is it possible that someone is spreading false rumors?"

"Why would anyone do that?" Luke said.

"If she was having an affair, especially for years, there are telltale signs. But no one knows who this person is."

"Have you asked Mary Madden?"

"The costume shop owner?"

"Yes, Mary knows everything happening in town. She always has the details before the details show up in the newspaper."

I was impressed. Mary must have an extensive network of friends and family. But could this also mean she could use the rumor mill to her advantage? "What if someone was spreading this rumor to ruin Fiona's reputation?"

"Fiona wasn't well-liked in the community. Her reputation couldn't get any worse. So I don't see why anyone would bother."

"The murderer?"

Luke frowned. "Now that's a scary thought."

"Who was Mary's husband?"

"She's single."

"I meant her late husband."

"She was engaged once, but she never got married."

I had assumed Mary Madden was a young widow because she was part of my aunt's Survivors Club. "Who was she engaged to and when?"

"Juan Perez. Over a decade ago when Mary was in her twenties."

"Fiona's husband? Our number one suspect?"

"One and the same."

"What happened?"

"They'd just gotten engaged, and then Juan got Fiona pregnant, one of those one-night stand situations. If Juan hadn't shown up at the wedding altar for Fiona, Malcolm probably would have broken both of Juan's legs."

I blinked, processing what I had just heard. Was the Hispanic man in the photo I'd seen in the costume shop Juan? Why would a sane person want a daily reminder of a broken engagement? "What if Mary killed Fiona for revenge? Or what if she was still in love with Juan? He was the one that got away."

Luke gave me an incredulous look. "Have you seen the guy?"

"I've seen an old photo in the costume shop's

backroom. He was decent looking years ago. And everyone is entitled to their taste—good or bad."

"Obviously, you must have bad taste if you think anyone would be pining over Juan."

I narrowed my eyes at Luke. What was his problem?

Luke put everything back into Fiona's purse. "What do you think I should do with this?"

"You should put it back where you found it."

"You're not helping me?"

"What does this have to do with me?" I said.

"I stole it for your aunt."

"I thought you said borrow."

Luke gave me a deadpan expression. "Are you helping or not?"

I chewed my lower lip. "We can't hold on to the purse."

"Can you distract Chrissy again?"

I shook my head. "She was already suspicious when you left the kitchen so abruptly. Maybe we should hand the purse over to the police. They need to know about the divorce papers. It might be a clue."

"And get charged for tampering with the evidence?" Luke shook his head. "No way. Sometimes Everly can get petty."

"Then what do you suggest we do?" I asked. "Take it with us? I need to go talk to Mary Madden and see how she'll react to the news of the divorce papers."

"Let's take it with us for now," Luke said, holding the purse out to me.

"I'm not touching that. We're in enough trouble already with Aunt Coco in jail."

Luke gave me a pleading look. "It's a lady's purse."

"And you look very manly with it," I said.

We strolled out of the tea shop, and I locked the front door. As I opened my truck door, I realized Luke was still next to me. "What are you doing?"

"I'm coming with you."

I shook my head. "I don't think so. There's no room in my tiny truck. I plan to pick up my aunt after the interview with Mary."

Luke glanced down at my heels. "I don't know why women wear such stupid shoes," he muttered under his breath.

He had a point, but I was still annoyed with his voicing the thought out loud. I lifted my chin. "It gives me a polished look."

Luke turned away from me, strolling toward his vehicle. "We can take my truck."

It was bad enough that I had two armchair detectives in the form of Aunt Coco and Babcia, but now it looked like I was saddled with another one. I sighed. I didn't have the energy to argue with him.

We piled into Luke's truck. I probably should feel bad for wasting his gas, since Mary's costume shop was three blocks away. Before my divorce, I would have insisted we walk and nurse my aching feet afterwards when I was alone. I wasn't sure why, but I didn't feel the need to be accommodating in front of Luke. Probably because I knew he didn't care for me, so it didn't matter what I did. And I was okay with this.

Luke parked next to the other trucks and vans in front of the bar even though there were plenty of spots in front of the costume shop. His vehicle blended in, and we headed over to the shop next door.

When we stepped into the costume shop, Mary Madden was ringing up a customer. I pretended to browse the rack, while keeping an eye on the conversation at the cash register. Once again, Luke blended in with the background and snooped around the shop. He must have been a spy in a previous life. From the corner of my eye, I saw him disappear behind the beaded curtain to the back room. I hope he didn't have a habit of "borrowing" things from people.

Mary wore a red cat suit with black stitching that was more obscene than nudity. She completed the outfit with a cat-ears headband and a tail. She finished up her transaction, and strutted over to greet me. As she moved, the tight fabric highlighted crevices that should have remained unseen. With the lack of air circulation from the outfit, how often did she have to deal with yeast infections?

I focused my eyes on Mary's forehead. If I met her gaze, I would burst out laughing.

"Hi, Cedar. How can I help you?" Mary glanced around the store. "Wasn't someone with you?"

I ignored Mary's question. If she hadn't noticed Luke, I wasn't giving him away. "Have you heard about my aunt?"

Mary's gaze was still focused on the rest of the store, and she reluctantly returned her attention to me. "No, what happened?"

"She's being charged for Fiona's murder," I said bluntly.

Mary gasped, eyes widening and both hands flew to her mouth. I couldn't tell if she meant it, or was just a good actress. "That's outrageous. I'm contacting the Survivors Club. And we will hold a rally outside the police station until they release Coco."

I felt guilty for suspecting Mary, but I had to be sure I could trust her. Since my aunt's arrest, I felt like I went through a carnival fun house. Folks who I had initially thought were friends could be foes, and enemies could be my allies. It was strange and unsettling.

"My aunt could use all the support she can get from the community," I said. "However, I am far more concerned about catching the real killer."

At my mention of the investigation, Mary's attitude shifted ever so slightly. All of a sudden, the friendly smile became more brittle. I was crossing over to a more dangerous territory and probably pressing my luck.

My heart rate sped up, and I felt uneasy. If Mary were the real killer, then I might be baiting the bear. Luckily, Luke was somewhere in the store. And if I screamed my head off, I was sure he would hear me and come running.

"Cedar, you should leave Fiona's murder to the police," Mary said. "Coco would be devastated if something were to happen to you."

I licked my lower lip, fighting the urge to resume the good girl role. Was Mary threatening me? Or was

I reading too much into this brief warning? "I've been hearing things about you and Juan Perez. That the two of you were once engaged, and he left you to marry a pregnant Fiona."

Mary paled, and her mouth clamped together tightly in a straight line. She regarded me coldly before finally letting out an exasperated sigh. "I knew this would come up sooner or later," she muttered under her breath.

Clearing her throat to compose herself once more, Mary looked away briefly before returning her gaze to mine. "Yes, Juan and I were once engaged." Her tone was forlorn like this topic dredged up painful memories she had yet to heal from.

I waited, but Mary didn't offer any further details or explanation. After a long moment of silence, I asked, "Were you upset with him? Upset enough to kill his wife?"

Mary's expression turned dark. "No!" She narrowed her gaze at me, and I could feel the force of her anger directed at me. "I loved Juan! I would never harm him or his wife. He left me because he wanted a different kind of life, and I couldn't give it to him. I never wanted children."

I made an encouraging noise, hoping she would keep talking.

"You have no idea how it feels to be cast aside for someone else," Mary continued. "It hurts, but we would probably have gotten divorced eventually because Juan wanted children. We wanted different things in life." The words came out sincere and heartfelt. She stopped her rant and took a deep breath. "But I'm over it." She gestured around the shop. "And the girls in the Survivors Club are helping me."

I nodded to acknowledge her words. They were the right words, but I didn't believe them. Her failed engagement was over a decade ago, and she said the book club was helping her now. That didn't sound like someone who had gotten over it. "Did you know that Fiona was planning to divorce Juan?"

For half a second, the corner of Mary's lips curled before she quickly recomposed herself. "No. I didn't know."

"Fiona wanted to divorce Juan but died before she could do so," I said.

"How do you know this?" Mary asked. Her tone was casual enough, but from her intense look, I could tell she was hanging onto my every word.

I hesitated, not sure if I should reveal my source.

*Crash!*

The two of us swiveled our gazes to the beaded

curtain leading to the back room. After half a heart-beat, Mary sprang into action. She ran over to the cash register and drew the katana mounted behind the countertop.

Before I could even process what happened, the shop owner was already pushing aside the beaded curtain with the sharp Japanese sword. From the way Mary moved with the sword in her hand, I could tell it wasn't a prop. Mary was an expert swordswoman.

## 16

## STRAW DOLLS

With my heart in my throat, I ran after Mary.

*Bam!*

Footsteps clattered.

Mary screamed in frustration. Had the costume shop owner gone berserk?

*Bam!*

I swiped aside the beaded curtain to find an empty back room. My gaze swept through the storage space, scanning for movement. I flung open the door across the room. It opened to the back of the shops and a gravel parking lot with a dumpster.

Mary stood in the middle of the parking lot, with her chest heaving and the Japanese sword clenched in her fist. Her face was red with rage. I shivered in fear and ducked back into the costume shop.

I stood still, waiting for my eyes to adjust to the sudden dimness. What was that thing in the corner? Why would someone put a black box on the floor? I hadn't noticed it previously because it was covered by a black cloth that was now a puddle on the concrete floor. And when the restroom door was open, it blocked the altar from view. I kneeled down to get a closer look and gasped.

It was nothing like the altar in traditional Chinese homes where they give offerings to their ancestors and ask for blessings. Nor was it like the shrine to the land deity seen in some Chinese shops to bless the physical space of their business.

No, this altar was to evoke a darker force. The dark-colored box held two roughly made straw dolls tied together by red string. I couldn't make out the words on the strip of yellow paper glued to the dolls' torsos. One doll had dark hair glued to its head, and the other doll had several blonde hairs wrapped around its head. The hair appeared to be real human hair. The blonde doll was covered with a liquid that looked like dried blood.

The altar was an eerie sight, and I shivered again. I got up and stumbled out of the shop, my heart pounding in my chest. I broke a heel on the board-walk and fell. I got up and limped over to Luke's truck. I tried the door, but it was locked. Breathing heavily, I ducked low and kept my gaze on the shop door.

Mary popped her head out of the shop, but luck-ily, she wasn't holding the sword anymore. Her face was still flush, but her expression was pleasant. I wasn't falling for the normal shop owner persona again. The woman was crazy.

Luke came out of the twenty-four-hour conve-nience store, holding a supersize fountain drink and a plastic bag. He saw me huddling next to his passenger door where Mary could not see me. His gaze casually swiveled over to Mary, and he nodded in acknowledgment. The shop owner narrowed her eyes at him, probably wondering if she had seen Luke come inside the costume shop with me.

He ignored Mary's inquisitive look and remotely unlocked the truck doors. I got in the same time he did, ducking low into my seat. He took off his blue parka and draped it over my head. By the time he started the car engine and backed out of the parking lot, Mary had already gone back into her shop.

When we rounded the block, I straightened up and sighed in relief. My ankle ached, but I ignored it.

I studied Luke's profile. "Why were you making all that noise in the back room?"

Luke kept his eyes on the road, but his cheeks reddened. "I was startled by something and knocked over a mannequin."

"Was it the straw dolls?" I asked.

Luke glanced at me and then back at the road. "Every culture has their version of cursing others, and the Japanese use a straw doll called a wara ningyo that serves the same purpose as a voodoo doll. But I'd never before seen it done in real life." His mouth twisted in distaste. "I touched the blood, and it's real."

"Is Mary half Japanese?"

"I think her grandmother is Japanese."

"I got Mary all worked up from my questions, and when she heard the noise, she came after you with a katana."

Luke grimaced. "Then it's lucky I got away."

"Did you find out anything else?" I asked.

"The name on the bloody straw doll is Fiona."

THE SOUND of a ringing cell phone filled the air. First, the ringing came from inside my purse, and then the ringing came from inside Luke's pocket. He pulled over and parked next to the curb. He got out and answered his call.

I pulled out Aunt Coco's cell phone and checked the display. "Hi, Perry. Do you have any news?"

"We are almost done posting bail. Do you want to pick up your aunt, or do you want me to drive her home?" the lawyer said.

I did a fist pump in the air. "That was fast."

"Apparently, the judge went to school with Gabriel Woods."

My heart lightened at the thought of my late uncle looking out for my aunt. "I'll be there in ten minutes."

When Luke got back into the truck, I said, "I need to go pick up my aunt at the police station."

"I just spoke to Josh," Luke said. "He was confirming his flight information. I'm picking him up from the airport tomorrow."

Was it the weekend already? I barely got to town. "I wonder why he didn't call me to pick him up."

Luke raised an eyebrow. "If you want to get up at five o'clock in the morning, be my guest."

Never mind. My brother didn't want his little sister up before the rooster. I patted Luke's shoulder. "Thank you for the sacrifice. I owe you one."

"Don't worry. I plan to collect."

Luke drove us to the police station. I studied Luke's profile from the corner of my eye. I wasn't sure what to make of his last comment. When we first met, he didn't particularly care for me, but maybe he was now warming up to me. Since it appeared that he was a family friend to the rest of my family, it would make our future interactions uncomfortable if he didn't at least tolerate me. We didn't have to be friends, but I didn't like the idea of Luke actively disliking me.

"Stop overthinking it," Luke said. "I can hear the gears turning in your head."

I blushed. How did he know what I was thinking about? "I don't know what you're talking about."

"Josh said you had a habit of overanalyzing everything to death. We'll tell Everly about the voodoo dolls, and she will take care of it. Just sit back and enjoy the ride. We'll be at the police station soon enough."

Luke thought I was still thinking about the murder investigation. I better keep up with the farce. "I can't help it. I don't know what I will do if my aunt ends up in jail for Fiona's murder."

"It won't come to that. We might have a small police force, but Everly is good at her job."

There he went again. Was there something he knew that I didn't know? "What's the nature of your relationship with Chief Blunt? Are you two friends or something else?"

His gaze met mine for a brief moment, and the corner of his lips curled. "Why? Are you jealous?"

I scoffed at his answer and rolled my eyes, my heart hammering loudly. "What makes you so confident she would keep digging for the truth?"

The amusement slipped off his face. "I have known Everly since forever. When you grow up in a small town like this, everybody knows everybody. Everly will do her job. She wants to be just like her dad."

I disagreed with Luke but didn't see the point in arguing. I didn't have faith that a once troublemaker was now a pillar of the community. After all, if Chief Blunt were doing her job, she wouldn't have charged my aunt in the first place. "I thought her dad sold boats."

"That was her stepdad. Her real dad was a police chief in Washington state."

I blinked. This was news to me. Had I been biased all this time because of something that happened in the playground all those years ago?

"The two of you are very similar," Luke continued.

"Who are you talking about?"

"You and Everly."

I snorted. This man didn't know what he was talking about.

Luke parked in front of the police station. As we got out, we ran into Chief Blunt coming out of Town Hall.

Before we could exchange greetings, Luke pulled out the black purse from inside his parka and thrust it into Chief Blunt's hands. "I found this in the pantry of the coffee shop. It's Fiona's purse."

Chief Blunt looked stunned. She quickly opened the purse and examined its contents with a confused expression, as if she had expected something else inside. After a few moments of silence, Chief Blunt finally spoke. "Where did you find it?"

Luke explained that we had found the purse in the pantry at the coffee shop. He said we thought it was an odd place for a purse and grabbed it before it disappeared. "Not saying the cleaning lady was a thief, but there seems to be a lot of foot traffic in and out of the shop."

I was impressed with Luke's story. He made us out to be heroes rather than thieves. I nodded at the appropriate moments and hoped I had a helpful look on my face—just another Good Samaritan trying to help the police out.

When Luke finished speaking, Chief Blunt seemed to have come to a decision about our discovery. She gave us an appraising look before thanking us for our help. "I'll get in touch if I need anything else from you. Coco is waiting for you inside." She held the front door of the police station open for us.

I poked Luke in the side with my elbow and whispered, "Voodoo dolls."

"One more thing, Everly." Luke told Chief Blunt what we found in the backroom of Mary Madden's costume shop.

Chief Blunt listened with an impassive face. She thanked us for the information and strolled into her office. Once she was out of earshot, both Luke and I breathed a sigh of relief.

Luke caught my eye and smiled. "Problem solved."

If it had been me, Evil Bun wouldn't have let me off that easily.

Marshall waved to us from the front counter. "I'll get Coco for you." He slid off the stool and shuffled across the room to the door on the left.

I turned to Luke. "I thought we were holding onto the purse until we figured out what to do."

"Did you see the way Everly looked at me? It was like she could see into my soul." Luke shivered. "I freaked out and just wanted to come clean."

I studied the tall, fit man next to me. Was he for real? I made a mental note never to let Luke in on anything that could be borderline illegal. With his blabbermouth, he was bound to tell everything to Evil Bun. And here I thought I was the goody two shoes.

A door banged, and I glanced at the source of the noise.

Aunt Coco marched into the room. "I'm so hungry. I could eat a horse. I can't believe they don't feed you in jail."

"You weren't in jail," Marshall said. "You were in a holding cell. And I offered you oatmeal this morning, but you refused."

Aunt Coco snorted in disgust. "You call that breakfast? That's the kind of stuff you use to remove paint." She caught sight of me and waved enthusiastically. "Cedar Bear, I am starving."

"Let's go to Hazel's for lunch," Luke said.

"Skywalker, you're my hero," Aunt Coco said, hands on her heart.

I rolled my eyes. My aunt was such a drama queen sometimes. "Do we have to sign any forms?" I asked Marshall.

The volunteer clerk shook his head. "Perry took care of everything. Have a good weekend."

The next two days would probably turn out to be unpleasant. My brother was on his way home from his conference. When I explained the murder situation to him, he would blow a gasket. And more likely than not, he would forbid us from investigating Fiona's death. We were running out of time.

## 17

### BUSTED

Once we were in Luke's truck, Aunt Coco said, "I need to go home to wash away the stink of jail and tell your uncle that I'm okay."

Luke gave me a quizzical look, and I shrugged. I didn't want to get into the explanation about my uncle's reincarnated spirit. I was surprised he didn't know about this already. Maybe Aunt Coco saved her wackiest ideas for the family.

I gave my aunt her cell phone, and she happily checked in with her friends online.

"The Survivors Club was planning to have a rally in front of the police station this evening on my behalf." Aunt Coco's fingers danced across her screen. "I better tell them I got out of jail."

Luke dropped us off in front of my aunt's house and said he would return with sandwiches shortly.

No white cargo van was watching the house, and I breathed a little easier.

While my aunt ran upstairs to shower, I went next door to look for General. I tried Babcia's back door, and it was unlocked. I was still getting used to folks leaving their doors unlocked. Back in San Jose, not only did we lock our doors, most of our windows were closed as well, relying on the HVAC to bring in fresh air.

Babcia was at the sink, washing dishes. "Is Coco back yet? Do you need lunch?"

"Aunt Coco is taking a shower, and Luke is getting sandwiches," I said. "Want to join us for lunch?"

Babcia shook her head. "I just finished. I'm going down for a nap after this. But, boy, it's been a busy night, and I'm exhausted."

I grabbed General's leash from the hook next to the back door. "Is the rascal here somewhere?"

"You didn't see him in the backyard when you came over?"

"Is he with Huntley?"

Babcia shook her head. "He dashed out of here

about ten minutes ago. I thought maybe he was chasing a squirrel or something."

I frowned.

"Don't worry. Both your aunt's yard and mine are completely fenced in. General wouldn't get out. He might be back home already."

I thanked Babcia for her help, opened the back door, and stepped outside.

"General," I called out.

No answer.

The only sound was the distant hum of cars passing by on Main Street and the chatter of birds in the trees.

I wandered around the yards, looking under bushes and trees, but still, there was no sign of him. At times like this, I wished the dog could talk.

At my aunt's yard, I called for him again.

No answer.

I bit my lower lip. Should I or shouldn't I? If it worked, so what if I embarrassed myself? No one was around to hear me.

I cupped my hands around my mouth. "Uncle Gabriel!" I felt silly, but it was worth a try. I didn't have anything else. "Uncle Gabriel, it's Cedar."

A few seconds later, I heard a bark and a series of yips from behind me. I whirled around. And there he was—General, prancing like he was in a parade. My heart leaped with joy. I didn't want to admit it to myself, but I was half expecting an afternoon of posting missing dog flyers.

I walked over to General and clipped on his leash. His ears twitched as if he was trying to tell me something important. He looked at me expectantly, his big brown eyes filled with curiosity. Clipped onto his green beret was a tiny yellow scroll.

I patted him affectionately on the head and removed the paper. The note was written in block letters on yellow legal pad paper. It was wrinkled and worn as if it had gone through the washing machine. Did the writer want to wash away finger-prints? Without my reading glasses, I held the paper an arm's length away to make out the words.

*Stop looking into Fiona's death or you're next.*

I shivered at the threatening note. My eyes scanned the yard, looking for any suspicious activity. Nothing seemed out of place. Was someone threat-ening to hurt my aunt's dog? Or was someone threat-ening me or my aunt?

General tugged at his leash, his brown eyes

telling me not to worry. How did I know this? I couldn't say, but I felt comforted. There were enough strange things happening since I'd been home that talking to the family pet and expecting an answer felt perfectly normal. I tucked the note into my pocket, crossed the yard with General, and returned to my aunt's back door.

Aunt Coco and Luke were at the dining room table. My aunt had already taken a few bites of her tuna salad sandwich. She dropped the sandwich on the waxed paper and flung herself at the corgi.

"General!" Aunt Coco hugged the dog and kissed his head. The dog gave me a long-suffering look but sat still. I had seen that look on my Uncle Gabriel's face plenty of times in my childhood. Eventually, my aunt unclipped his leash and carried him to the laundry room to feed him. Apparently, feeding her dog was more important than feeding herself.

I went into the kitchen and washed my hands. As I took a seat at the dining room table, I thanked Luke for picking up lunch.

Luke waved away my thanks. "Are you okay? You look like you've seen a ghost."

I choked on the bite of the ham sandwich, the bread sticking to the back of my throat. I grabbed a glass of water and downed it, dislodging the piece of food. Luke bolted out of his chair and pounded my back.

"I'm okay," I finally managed to gasp out.

Luke hovered over me like he didn't believe me.

I took a deep breath and said in a normal voice. "I'm fine. Sit down." I pulled out the note from my pocket. "Someone left this for us."

As Luke read the note, he frowned. "This could be serious. Who knew you were looking into Fiona's death?"

I grimaced. Maybe I should have kept my mouth shut. In hindsight, using myself as bait to lure out the killer was a stupid idea. "Everyone—with the way news travels around town."

Luke handed the note back to me. "Yeah, I can see that."

I slapped my forehead. "Holy macaroni. Now both our fingerprints are on the note."

Luke blinked at me, and the corner of his mouth twitched. I started chuckling, not quite sure why I found the situation funny. He joined me, and the two of us laughed until I had tears. We probably needed to release the tension. When I finally wiped the tears from my eyes, I felt much better. I wasn't alone and didn't have to manage things on my own.

I put the note back in my pocket. "Don't tell

Aunt Coco. She already has enough on her plate. I don't want her to worry about the note, especially because it was found on General's beret."

"But if she doesn't know about the threat, she could get into trouble."

I gave him a deadpan look. "She's already in trouble. We'll just keep an eye on her. Make sure she's not alone."

Luke hesitantly nodded.

Aunt Coco came back and picked up her sandwich. "Anything happen while I was in the slammer?"

I met Luke's gaze, and he gave me a slight nod as if to say I get to decide what to tell my aunt. I told my aunt about finding Fiona's purse and the divorce papers.

Aunt Coco's jaw dropped. "This is like a soap opera. I wonder if she was divorcing her husband to marry her lover."

"Maybe there is no lover," I said. "It's all a case of smoke and mirrors."

Aunt Coco reluctantly nodded. "If Mary Madden doesn't know who this person is, then he probably doesn't exist."

"Why go through all the trouble of spreading

this rumor?" Luke said. "It seems like such a waste of time."

"Maybe someone has nothing better to do with their time," Aunt Coco said.

I wasn't sure it was idle chatter, but there wasn't much I could do about it at the moment. Better to focus on what I could control. "Let's finish lunch and then find Juan for a chat," I said. "Do you know where he lives?"

"He's not home," Luke said. "I saw him at the used car dealership this morning."

"But his wife..." I trailed off, not wanting to say "was murdered" out loud. "Passed away." Even though there were problems in the marriage, why wasn't the husband at home mourning for Fiona?

Luke shrugged.

I told my aunt about Juan and Mary's engagement and finding the Japanese wara ningyo. "It was eerie. If it had been voodoo dolls, I would have been less scared because they are commercialized. But these straw dolls felt ancient and real. I didn't want anything to do with it."

"I didn't know Juan and Mary were once engaged," Aunt Coco said. "I wonder why she never mentioned it."

"How well do you know Mary?" I asked

"We've been friends for over a year. I thought I knew her well enough, but now, I'm not so sure."

"Do you know why she is in the Survivors Club? Who did she lose?"

Aunt Coco frowned. "I don't recall. But I was under the impression that she's a young widow."

My heart sank. I had liked the costume shop owner when I first met her. "What if she thought of herself as a widow because Juan left her for Fiona?"

"That's crazy talk. All of us have to deal with breakups at one point or another. You can't get through life without kissing a few frogs."

"Exactly." I ticked the points off on my fingers. "Crazy. Obsessive."

Aunt Coco shook her head. "I still don't believe it."

Luke set his glass of iced tea down. "Normal people don't go around cursing a romantic rival from over a decade ago. There's something wrong with that woman."

For the next few minutes, we ate in silence. There wasn't much left to say until we got more evidence. I sipped my water between bites and felt a moment of pure joy. Sure, there was still a lot of uncertainty and the possibility of jail time, but I was with my aunt and a family friend. For the first time since I decided to return home, I felt like I had made the right choice.

I didn't have to put on a façade that I was okay when everything was falling apart around me like I did with my so-called "friends" in San Jose. It felt nice to be myself for a change.

WE FINISHED OUR SANDWICHES, but before we could leave the house, Aunt Coco insisted that we put on our costumes again. Instead of subjecting Luke to my aunt's logic about how the costumes were a walking advertisement for the tea shop, I went upstairs to change. I was too happy to have my aunt back to argue with her. While my aunt and I changed, Luke took General out for a walk to take care of his doggie business.

A few minutes later, we left General home with the pet door closed. I didn't want someone to kidnap General while we were away. Luckily, Aunt Coco didn't question me about the pet door. We got into Luke's truck. It was a bench seat, and I sat uncomfortably between my aunt and Luke. He drove to the outskirts of town, towards the light industrial area where Juan's dealership was located. We drove in silence, lost in our thoughts.

Before we even got out of the car, several sales-people made a beeline for us. I left Aunt Coco and Luke to fend them off, and I strolled around the group to the modular trailer that served as an office.

I climbed up the metal steps and cautiously opened the door, unsure of what to expect. The desk closest to the door was empty. The receptionist was nowhere in sight. The rest of the space was divided into cubicles with six-foot gray walls. Luckily, I was short enough that no one would see my head above the cubi-cle. Since Juan was the used car dealership owner, he probably had the largest office space by a window.

I slowly made my way around the perimeter of the trailer, looking at the name tags. The air was thick with the smell of stale coffee and the cloying sweetness of a pastry box, probably donuts. My heart pounded against my chest, not from fear, but from excitement. I couldn't remember the last time I had felt this alive and present in the moment.

Even if I was caught, what was the worst thing that could happen? I wasn't stealing or vandalizing anything. I had always been the good girl, afraid I would lose my adopted parents' love. This goody-two-shoes behavior got even worse when I lived with my aunt because my cousins were always getting into trouble, and I was the "good one." But now, I had nothing to lose.

I stood still for a moment, blinking at a sudden thought. If my family didn't want me, they would have already discarded me decades ago. Why had this never occurred to me before? Would I have left my failing marriage rather than wait for my ex-husband to get rid of me? Was I afraid what I'd had with him was all I deserved? That I wouldn't get any more in another relationship? I shook my head. This wasn't the place for such deep thoughts.

The finance woman was with two customers and didn't even look up when I walked past the opening of her cubicle. Up ahead, in the corner, was an enclosed office space with a door. I glanced up at the nameplate and wasn't surprised to see Juan's name etched on the plastic.

Before I got a chance to knock, I heard a man talking. I pressed my ear to the door, and surprisingly, heard the conversation like I was in the room. There was no sound insulation.

"I can't keep doing this anymore," Juan said, his voice heavy with exhaustion.

Silence.

No one responded, which meant Juan must be on the phone.

"I need to figure out what will be best for my son," Juan said.

Silence.

Juan finally whispered, "Christ, he just lost his mother. Give me some time."

Silence.

I debated what to do next. All this effort to eavesdrop, and I got nothing from it. I hated only knowing half of the conversation. Should I knock on the door? Or should I let Juan have his privacy?

"What are you doing?" a woman's voice called out from behind me. "And what is that awful smell?"

I spun around to find the finance woman standing outside her cubicle, holding a mug, her face full of suspicion. My mind went blank. I wasn't good at lying on the fly. If I had thought of an excuse ahead of time, I could say it at the appropriate moment. As it was, my tongue felt heavy and thick. I was so busted.

## 18

## MORE FINGER POINTING

"There you are," Aunt Coco called out from the doorway. "How long does it take to go to the bathroom?"

Holy macaroni. My aunt gave me the perfect excuse. I pressed my hands around my stomach. "I told you there was something wrong with the eggs."

It was just my luck that Luke stepped into the trailer as I pretended to groan. His bemused gaze swiveled between my aunt and me.

The finance woman wrinkled her nose and took a step back. "Haven't you heard of the courtesy flush?"

Heat rose from my chest to engulf my head. If only a hole would open up on the ground and swallow me. I was too old for this kind of stuff to happen to me.

I glanced at Luke, and one corner of his mouth curled up as if he was trying to suppress a smile. Henceforth, he would probably think of me as "Cedar Poop Master."

Juan opened his office door. "Everything okay out here?" His voice was gruff like he was experiencing some deep emotion. Maybe he was grieving for his wife in his own way.

He was in his late thirties, so it was a May-December relationship with Fiona almost a decade older than him. His brown eyes were bloodshot, and his black hair was unkempt and patchy. I didn't need to be a fortune teller to know hair loss was in his future. His suit jacket was rumpled, and the top buttons of his shirt were undone. I wasn't sure why he needed to be in the office today, but it was obvious he shouldn't be here.

The finance woman took one look at her boss and quickly retreated into her cubicle. Smart woman.

Juan's gaze landed on my aunt, and he did a double take, probably at the Mad Hatter costume. He blinked and shook his head. "Coco, now is not the time to complain about my late wife."

"We aren't here to complain." Aunt Coco's voice was soft and gentle. It was a stark contrast to the way she'd spoken before. "We came to check on you."

"I can't talk right now," Juan said. "I have to finish the payroll and get home to my son."

"What will happen to the coffee shop?" Aunt Coco asked. "Is Chrissy going to run it for you?"

Juan's mouth twisted into a bitter smile. "I don't get to make this decision. My dear wife appointed her nephew, Duncan, as the custodian of my son's trust. Apparently, she didn't think I could handle the money. Even in death, she had to twist the knife."

Since I hadn't been introduced, I didn't want to intrude on the conversation and break the temporary rapport between my aunt and Juan. Even Luke appeared frozen by the wall as if to blend in with the furnishings. He probably knew the slightest movement would break the enchantment, and Juan would clam up.

I couldn't help but compare Fiona's marriage with my own. She had held the purse strings, and even in death, she played the tune for Juan. Yet, while she seemed more empowered than me, I wondered if she was any happier.

My marriage had been more like a roommate situation by the end, with both of us going through the motions for the sake of appearances. We weren't unhappy, so I had thought we were fine. Subconsciously, I must have kept a busy schedule so I didn't have to think or feel anything. Staying busy was an avoidance tactic, but it couldn't last forever.

"The two of you have been married for over a decade," Aunt Coco pointed out. "Is there a life insurance policy? I can't imagine she would leave you with nothing."

"Nothing," Juan said. "I got nothing."

I wondered if Juan thought his marriage to Fiona was fine. Something had kept them together, even if both of them were miserable. Perhaps their son.

"But the dealership is yours, right?" Aunt Coco said.

"No, my father-in-law owns the dealership," Juan said bitterly. "I'm just the wrench monkey that keeps things running."

Aunt Coco mumbled something incoherent in a soothing tone.

I poked my aunt with my elbow. "Fiona's lover," I whispered.

Aunt Coco stared at me blankly.

I bent my head closer to her ear. "Ask him who is Fiona's lover."

I must have spoken louder than I intended.

Juan's gaze shifted between Aunt Coco and me. His voice was hoarse when he said, "What are you talking about? There's no lover."

"Who do you think killed your wife?" Aunt Coco said.

"There is no lover," he said firmly.

I cocked my head and studied Juan. Was denial a machismo behavior? Maybe this was why he'd stayed with his wife all these years. He couldn't come to terms with his wife's cheating...or maybe Juan was telling the truth?

"There's a rumor that Fiona has been cheating on you for years," I said. "Do you know about that?"

Juan shifted his gaze to me. His expression became guarded. "Who are you?"

"I am Cedar Woods. Coco's niece." I didn't stick out my hand because he probably wouldn't shake it. "Do you know why someone would spread a rumor about your wife's infidelity?"

"That's enough," he said in a low voice.

The hair on the back of my neck stiffened at the underlying anger in Juan's voice.

"My wife was a good woman," Juan continued. "People need to stop spreading this malicious lie."

The words sounded appropriate, given the situation, but did he mean it? After all, he could say whatever he wanted now that his wife was gone. Or maybe this was guilt talking? Did he have something to do with his wife's death?

Aunt Coco shot me a look as if this was all my fault. She made some soothing noise, but Juan wasn't having it.

Juan balled up his hands into fists, and his breathing came in rapid, shallow breaths. "The two of you need to leave."

I eyed him warily. Maybe he would crack if we played the tough cop card. "If no one has a reason for killing Fiona, then you will become the fall guy."

Juan laughed scornfully. "Isn't Coco charged for Fiona's murder?"

"It won't stick," I said firmly, cutting off his laughter. "After the judge examines the so-called evidence, he'll throw out the case. Besides, the spouse is always the prime suspect in these situations. Once the police are done with my aunt, they'll come after you next."

Juan winced like he had known it would come to this. He ran his hand through his hair, mulling over what I said. After a few moments of silence, he finally said, "I don't know who would want to kill my wife. Maybe this is in retaliation for my father-in-law."

"What do you mean?" I asked.

Juan gave me a pointed look. "Have you heard about Malcolm Spencer's shady business dealings?"

I nodded.

"What makes you think he doesn't have enemies waiting to take out his family? Fiona was his pride and joy."

I regarded Juan skeptically. I doubted that Fiona's death had anything to do with her father. If Malcolm Spencer was the local crime boss, he would surely have posted bodyguards around his family. Crime bosses didn't get to where they were at by being stupid.

And after Fiona's death, wouldn't Malcolm lock down the family, especially his grandson, until he figured out the next step? Nope, Fiona's killer came from someone closer to home. I gave Juan a sideways glance. Was he intentionally pointing the finger at his father-in-law? Or did he really have no clue who might want to kill his wife?

"What were you doing on the day Fiona died?" I asked.

"I dropped off my son for school, and then I went to the dealership," Juan said.

"But Kelly Hammer saw you skulking in the back alley behind the shops," Aunt Coco said.

My aunt's words jolted a memory loose. Ah, that was where I heard about the van. Could this be the same white van outside my aunt's house for the last few days?

Juan shook his head. "I didn't kill my wife."

"Then what were you doing in the back alley?" I said. "Kelly said you climbed into a white cargo van."

Juan backed away from us. "I don't need to talk to you. You aren't the police."

"Did you know that Fiona had already filled out divorce papers?" I said.

Juan turned ashen. "What?"

"The police found them in her purse," I said. Technically, Luke had found them, but Evil Bun probably knew about the papers by now.

Juan shook his head as if denying my words. He spun on his heels and bolted for his office, slamming the flimsy door shut.

I gaped at his reaction. He appeared genuinely shocked. Maybe he had no intention of divorcing his wife. Then Duncan's claim that Juan was willing to kill for his freedom wasn't true. But why would Juan point the finger at his father-in-law? Was he trying to throw us off the trail? Who was he trying to protect?

Aunt Coco took my elbow and steered me out of the trailer with Luke following closely behind. We didn't speak until we were outside in the sunlight with the trailer door shut firmly behind us.

"Where to now?" Luke asked.

"Home," Aunt Coco said, yawning. "I need a nap."

For a late fall day, the sun warmed my skin. I glanced at my aunt's exhausted face. We needed to get my truck, which was still parked outside the tea shop. But Old Town was close enough that this could wait.

As we walked back to Luke's truck, the salespeople watched us closely like a group of vultures waiting for one of us to dawdle behind. I hastened my steps to keep up with the others.

As Luke started the engine, he said, "What did Juan do for his late wife to hand over the financial reins to her nephew?"

Aunt Coco shrugged. "With Fiona gone, all we have is Juan's side of the story."

"And her father would naturally side with Fiona." I was curious and conflicted about the enigmatic Malcolm Spencer. He probably had information about his daughter, but if he was a mob boss, this could be a dangerous interview. It could wait until tomorrow. I yawned. My aunt wasn't the only one who'd had a sleepless night.

"I almost forgot, Coco," Luke said. "Malcolm Spencer wants to talk to you. He stopped by the sawmill earlier this morning, thinking I would know where he could find you."

"What did you tell him?" I asked.

"Same thing I told Everly yesterday. You'll go home eventually," Luke said.

"You told them to monitor my aunt's house," I said incredulously.

Luke looked sheepish. "Sorry, I might have given them the idea indirectly."

"Then don't take us home," Aunt Coco said.

"Where do you want to go?" Luke asked. "I can drop you off anywhere."

Aunt Coco raised an eyebrow at me. "What do you think, Cedar Bear?"

I hesitated, blushing at the use of my nickname. It was one thing for her to use my nickname when we were alone, but quite another around others. "Please drop us off a couple of blocks away, and we can do a reconnaissance before we approach the house."

"If Josh were here, he'd want me to take you to his house," Luke said.

I shook my head. "Even if he were here, his house is the last place we should go. Malcolm would know about Josh's connection to Aunt Coco."

"You can come to my house," Luke said.

I stopped breathing. It took all my willpower to drag my gaze from his eyes to stare at the road in front of us. I knew there was no innuendo implied in his comment, but my mind couldn't help but go down that path.

"We could go back to Old Town and take care of business," I said. "We need to call the contractor to resume the remodeling."

"I texted Kelly already." Aunt Coco yawned. "I need a nap. Spending a night in the slammer isn't as fun as when I was younger."

I gave my aunt a sideways glance. How come I hadn't heard about these escapades before? "Home it is. But don't drop us off at the front door. " If my aunt hadn't noticed the white cargo van, there was no point in worrying her. She had enough on her plate. "We could use a short walk."

Luke dropped us off two blocks away from Aunt Coco's house. He didn't ask any questions and said to call him if we needed anything else. I could get used to having an attractive man at my beck and call.

We walked in silence for several minutes. Aunt Coco was quiet, lacking her usual energy. I probably should have insisted Aunt Coco take a nap earlier rather than let her come with us to interview Juan.

We rounded the corner and I could see my aunt's house a block away. There was no police cruiser parked up front. Yay for small blessings. However, a white cargo van was parked at the alley's entrance behind my aunt's backyard. The sandwich I had earlier churned in my stomach.

I grabbed my aunt's hand and dragged her behind a Douglas fir.

"What is it?" Aunt Coco whispered. Her voice was more animated than before.

I pointed at the white vehicle. "It's that van again. The same one that was watching the house all day yesterday."

"This can't be good," Aunt Coco said.

I didn't see any movement coming from inside the van. Whoever was inside had been there long enough to be comfortable with their surroundings and felt secure enough that they didn't need to keep a constant eye on things outside. Otherwise, they would have already seen us coming around the corner of the block.

"How did Juan Perez get in front of us?" Aunt Coco said suddenly, snapping me out of my thoughts about the van's occupants.

"I don't think that's his van. Do you think it belongs to Malcolm or one of his goons?" I didn't know why we were whispering since we were too far away from the van for someone inside to hear us.

"I thought Kelly said Juan got into a white cargo van."

"But it doesn't mean Juan owns the van."

Aunt Coco nodded thoughtfully. "Then I guess it's time to make our move."

"What move?" I asked, not following my aunt's train of thought.

"We need to find out who is in that car," Aunt Coco said.

I nodded in agreement. But how were we going to pull this off without getting caught? We didn't have any masks, and there were no nearby bushes or trees big enough for us to hide behind without drawing attention. Even in our *Alice in Wonderland* costumes, it was easy enough to make out our faces.

Before I could stop her, Aunt Coco left the safety of the tree and darted down the street toward the van. I had no choice but to follow her.

## 19

## THE GODFATHER

I sprinted after my aunt, my adrenaline pumping through my veins. With outstretched arms, I reached out to grab the back of my aunt's jacket, but I only caught thin air.

Aunt Coco ran up to the van and rapped on the window. Two rough-looking men came out of the vehicle and flanked my aunt on either side. My heart almost gave out at the sight, and I pumped my legs even faster.

"What is going on here?" Aunt Coco demanded.

"Move along, granny," said one of the men, a bearded giant with a bald head. "We don't want any trouble here."

The second man—a thin, oily-haired man with

beady eyes—squinted at my aunt's face. "Wait a minute. Are you Coconut Woods?"

"It's Coco, as in Chanel, you nincompoop," Aunt Coco said. "Where did you get the nut from?"

I joined my aunt and pressed a hand to my side, trying to catch my breath. I was probably more hindrance than a help, but I clutched my purse, ready to whack one of them in the face with it.

"I don't know anything about Chanel," the giant goon said. "Why are you wearing an orange wig?" His gaze swiveled to me. "And a blonde wig? What are you two playing at?"

The thin goon rolled his eyes. "Will you get on with it? Who cares what they're wearing?"

The giant goon waved a finger at us. "If you don't want any trouble, you'll come with us."

Aunt Coco stood her ground and crossed her arms in defiance. "We're not going anywhere until you tell us who you are and why you're here," she said in a surprisingly calm voice, probably from raising four rambunctious boys.

The giant goon chuckled and turned to his oily-haired companion. "Looks like we've got a feisty granny on our hands."

The oily-haired goon sighed, apparently the

spokesman of the two. "We have been sent here by Malcolm Spencer. The boss wants to talk to you."

My breath came out in an audible swish. Talk was good. Nobody died when everyone kept talking.

The oily-haired goon gave me a stern look. "Now, you can choose whether we tie you up or you go willingly. But rest assured, one way or another, you're coming with us. The boss will get his answers."

My heart raced at the thought of being taken away by these two brutes. I frantically looked around for any sign of help. A few people were walking in the nearby streets, but none were close enough to have any chance of intervening in our situation.

Aunt Coco, however, seemed unfazed by the threat and pulled herself to her full height. "Let's go peacefully. It looks like Malcolm is back for more after our wonderful first date."

I gave my aunt a sideways glance. Was she delusional? Or maybe my aunt did have a friendly relationship with the Mirror Falls Godfather. Maybe this would all turn out okay.

The giant goon nodded and gestured for us to get into the van with a jerk of his head. I followed my aunt closely as she climbed in without hesitation. I felt like one of those stupid women in horror movies who knew they shouldn't go down to the basement or leave the safety of the house for the woods but did it anyway. But what else could I do? Let the goons drive off with my aunt?

We were taken to Malcolm's house, a luxurious estate on the outskirts of town. I thought this part of the county was mostly wooded federal land. However, as we wound up the mountain, I could see a handful of homes scattered around the base. Who owned these properties? Even if we screamed, they were too far away to help us.

We got out of the van. The guards stationed outside the well-manicured lawns did a double take. Probably because of the costumes. The two goons led us into the house and ushered us through the entrance into a large, opulent office that reeked of wealth and power.

It was decorated with fine art and mahogany furniture, and a thick Persian rug covered most of the marble floor. Malcolm sat in a leather armchair behind an imposing walnut desk. He regarded us with a grim expression and motioned for us to sit down on the two chairs before his desk. His two goons stood off to the side like loyal guard dogs.

"Coco," Malcolm said in his deep voice, "It's been a while."

I was surprised he didn't react to our costumes. Maybe he knew my aunt better than I thought.

Aunt Coco winked and blew him a kiss. "It has indeed."

My eyes widened. Holy macaroni. Did the first date at the waffle house actually happen?

Malcolm ignored the overture and fixed his gaze on Aunt Coco. "I heard you killed my daughter."

For a moment, all I could hear was the sound of my breathing. My heart felt like it would jump out of my chest. We were going to end up at the bottom of the lake. Why did my aunt approach the van?

Aunt Coco didn't seem perturbed by the accusation. Instead, she leaned back in her chair, her fingers steepled in front of her. "She wasn't yours."

Malcolm's face remained stoic and unreadable. His fingers drummed against his desk, and he eyed my aunt for a few moments. "This isn't a movie set."

Aunt Coco smiled at Malcolm. The silence stretched on while I wanted to scream from the tension. Finally, Malcolm motioned for his goons to leave the room.

The giant goon scowled at us. "Boss, what if the two try some funny business?"

Malcolm pulled a gun from a drawer and placed it on the desk.

I held up both hands, palms out. "There will be no funny business." I glanced at my aunt and gave her a pointed look. "No funny business."

Aunt Coco held up a hand as if she were swearing on a Bible and crossed her heart with a finger. I was not reassured.

The two henchmen left the room, and with the gun between Malcolm and us—the air was thick with tension.

Malcolm gave us a stern look, letting the silence intimidate us. It didn't affect my aunt. What did she know that I didn't?

Finally, Malcolm said, "I want to know who killed my girl."

"It wasn't me," Aunt Coco said.

"That's not what my contact at the police is saying," Malcolm said.

Aunt Coco waved her hand dismissively. "It wouldn't stick." She jerked a thumb in my direction. "And it's not my niece. She had no beef with Fiona."

Malcolm paused, considering her words. I held my breath, waiting for his verdict. Finally, he gave a slight nod. "I believe you."

I let out a sigh of relief.

"What have you discovered about my daughter's death?" he asked.

"I don't know what you mean," Aunt Coco replied coolly.

Malcolm's eyes narrowed. After a long pause, he said, "Don't try my patience, Coco. Now tell me what you know."

Aunt Coco remained silent, her eyes never leaving Malcolm. After another tense moment of silence, she finally broke it by speaking in an even voice, "I'm afraid I can't help you with that."

The muscles along Malcolm's jaw tightened visibly. A bead of sweat ran down the small of my back. The tension in the room was killing me. Malcolm was obviously pushed to the limits of his patience.

I raised my hand, feeling like I just laid my head on the chopping block. "Excuse me. How do you know we're investigating Fiona's death?"

Malcolm raised an eyebrow. "My people have been following you all day. From the moment you decided to run from the police, I knew you two were exactly what I needed."

I shivered at Malcolm's words. There was no point in suppressing my fear. Only a stupid woman —I gave my aunt a sideways glance—or a delusional one thought this was fun and games.

Aunt Coco preened. She covered her mouth with

a hand and leaned over to whisper, "I told you he has the hots for me."

I ignored her. "What exactly do you want from us?"

"I need you to investigate Fiona's death," Malcolm said.

I hadn't expected this answer. "We are not professional private investigators." I gestured at the opulent room. "Given your vast resources, you could do a better job than us."

"Apparently, the people in town are afraid to talk to my associates," Malcolm said. "And from what we have observed, they don't seem to be afraid of you two."

I sat back in my chair, the tension leaving me for the first time since I entered this room. "If we help you, what's in it for us?"

Malcolm raised an eyebrow. "You get to live another day."

I gave him a deadpan stare. Maybe he didn't understand the power had shifted in the room. From what I had learned from my ex-husband, this was now a business negotiation.

Aunt Coco opened her mouth, and I shot her a look. She pouted and crossed her arms, but thankfully, remained silent. I returned my gaze to

Malcolm. We had all the time in the world to wait him out.

Silence.

I shifted my gaze to a spot on his forehead. Staring into his deep green eyes was uncomfortable, and I didn't want to give away our upper hand.

Eventually, Malcolm sighed. "I can pay you."

We needed the money, but this meant once the transaction was done, it was done. While I didn't want to be in league with Malcolm, who knew what could happen in the future? The rumor mill said that he ran the town, and being on good terms with him might prove beneficial. "We don't want your money. Instead, we want a favor."

Malcolm blinked as if surprised that we were negotiating. "What do you want?"

"We don't know yet," I said. "This is for a future favor. If we are ever in need, we would like your help."

"So you want me to owe you?" Malcolm's voice took on a dangerous edge.

I stiffened my spine. Yes, Malcolm was intimidating, but he needed us, and this kept the fear at bay. If my aunt wasn't cowed by the power emanating from the man before us, I shouldn't be either. "I don't see it this way. Friends do nice things for each other all the time."

Malcolm studied me with a critical eye. "Are we friends?"

My heart gave a strange flutter at his words. I had been sheltered most of my life, so this was a completely different world. Friendships and loyalty here had more weight than what I had learned at the schoolyard. "You want to know what happened to Fiona, and so do we. This sort of makes us allies."

Malcolm tapped his fingers on his desk for a long moment. His gaze swiveled between my aunt and me.

I stared placidly back at him with my most non-threatening look. A smart person would tell Malcolm everything and hope this would be the last interaction with him. I guess I wasn't so smart.

"Deal," Malcolm finally said, dragging the word out like it hurt.

I glanced at Aunt Coco, who looked pleased. We both knew this was an offer we couldn't refuse. Malcolm and I sealed our deal with a handshake. The only way out of this friendship was through death. His or mine?

We told Malcolm what we had learned. I didn't think it was much, but he seemed satisfied.

"We'll keep you updated on further developments," I said.

"Give me your cell phone number," Malcolm said.

I shook my head. "My phone doesn't work here. No cell reception."

"I can give you my number," Aunt Coco said, holding up her phone.

Malcolm spoke into his smartwatch. The two goons came in, and the giant goon handed me a cell phone. Probably one of those untraceable phones. He gave me the phone's passcode.

"Keep it charged," Malcolm said. "I will call you."

"Can I use it to make personal calls?" I asked.

The two goons stared at me like I was soft in the head.

"Aren't you afraid I would listen in on your calls or read your text messages?" Malcolm asked.

I shrugged. If I had to be at the beck and call of the local crime boss, I might as well take advantage of the situation. It wasn't like I planned to use this phone for personal stuff. "If you want to listen to my conversations with my aunt or brother, go ahead."

Malcolm glanced at my aunt and back at me. "Be my guest."

The two goons hovered next to our elbows, ready to escort us out, but I stood my ground.

"We told you what we found out. Now it's your turn to enlighten us. What have you learned about your daughter's death? Who do you suspect?"

"If I suspected anyone, this person would be at the bottom of Trinity Lake," Malcolm said.

I shivered at his matter-of-fact tone. "Did you have a talk with Juan on the morning Fiona died?"

"How did you know?"

"Someone saw Juan getting in the van."

Malcolm shrugged. "What about it?"

"What was the conversation about?"

He stared at me unblinking for a long moment. "We were having a friendly chat. Sometimes a father has to do that with his son-in-law."

I raised an eyebrow. "Did he do something you disapproved of?"

"You could say that."

I sat up in my seat, considering his words. "This kind of conversation either involved Juan spending all the family money or another woman."

Malcolm's eyes widened.

"Since money did not appear to be an issue, Juan was seeing another woman." I was right all along. The rumor about Fiona's affair was all smoke and mirrors to divert the attention away from what Juan was doing.

"If I had proof, he would be dead meat."

Was this why Juan had looked so unkempt at the used car dealership? I had thought it was from grief over Fiona's death, but maybe it was from his come-to-Jesus moment with his father-in-law. "Who is he having an affair with?"

"I don't know, but Fiona had suspected he was no longer faithful. And after our talk, I hoped this was the end of it. If it weren't for my grandson, I would get rid of that mother"—Malcolm took a deep breath—"never mind."

"How long was your father and son chat?"

"If you're trying to find out if I can give Juan an alibi, then yes, I can provide one. He was with me until ten, but I left him at Trinity Lake, and that's an hour walk back into town."

"If someone had picked him up..."

Malcolm tilted his head at the goons. "I had my guys watching him to make sure he had to walk the whole way back...without shoes. It was his punishment for making me have to intervene. As much as I want to get rid of him, the loser is not the killer."

I thanked Malcolm for his time. It never hurt to be extra polite.

Malcolm dismissed us, and the two goons escorted us back into the van.

During the drive back to Aunt Coco's house, I wondered if this deal was playing with fire. We had left the place unscathed, and that was enough for now. But what if we couldn't uncover Fiona's killer? Would we end up at the bottom of Trinity Lake as punishment?

## 20

## TWILIGHT

When we opened the front door, General greeted us with a small whine. Aunt Coco scooped up her dog and headed upstairs for a nap. I followed after them and went into my room to change out of the Alice costume and into my regular attire of a hoodie with T-shirt underneath and sweatpants. I also took off my contacts and put on my glasses. My eyes were red and strained from wearing contacts all day.

I was ready to wind down with a nice dinner and a good book. I hadn't mentioned the sleepwalking to my aunt because I didn't want to worry her. Besides, there wasn't time for a heart-to-heart chat. From what I remembered, the therapist had said a bedtime routine would help me feel safe and thus prevent the sleepwalking. It was worth a try.

General padded in and bumped my leg.

"What is it boy?" I asked.

General tilted his head toward the doorway.

"Do you want to go for a walk?" I asked.

"Woof."

I took a deep breath. Had General remembered our previous conversation where I asked him to bark one for yes, and bark twice for no? "Are you a girl dog?"

General rolled his eyes up at the ceiling.

I blushed. "Humor me. I need to know if I am crazy. Are you a girl dog?"

"Woof. Woof."

I blinked and fell back onto the bed, my legs suddenly unable to support me. Was this for real? I watched General, his tail wagging, eagerly waiting for my next question. "Can you understand me?"

General barked once.

Shut the door. I was communicating with a dog. "Do you want to go for a walk?"

General barked once and padded to the doorway. He looked over his shoulder and his eyes asked me why I wasn't following his lead.

I licked my lower lip. "Uncle Gabriel?"

"Woof.'"

As I came to accept the impossible, tears began to well in my eyes. My aunt was right, and General was my uncle, the three-star general. The corgi might be a reincarnation, or he might be a guardian angel. It didn't matter which one it was. What mattered was that my uncle was back with us.

General padded over and licked my face. I hugged the corgi tightly, grateful for his presence. All the love that I had ever felt for Uncle Gabriel returned in full force, and I cried, letting out my hurt from the divorce and the fear of my aunt going to jail. Eventually, I took off my glasses to clean them on the hem of my shirt.

I walked General around the neighborhood so he could do his doggie business. We took our time, taking in all of the sights, sounds, and smells that we passed. Every now and then, I'd look down at General and our eyes would meet. I could feel the love radiating off of him as he walked by my side. His tail brushed against my leg as we walked, reminding me that no matter what happened, Uncle Gabriel still loved me and was always here for me.

When it was time to turn around, we stopped for

a few moments to take in all the beauty around us. The sun set behind the ponderosa pines, creating shadows. Birds sang sweet melodies from up high, and squirrels scampered through branches.

In this brief moment I felt closer to Uncle Gabriel than ever before, like he gave me a gift—a reminder that I always had a place in this family. I might have started out as an unwanted girl in a Chinese orphanage, but in the Woods family, not only was I loved, but I was the only girl. And since none of the boys were around, it was up to me to save my aunt.

AFTER AUNT COCO woke up from her nap, we gathered around Babcia's kitchen for the dumpling soup again. Apparently, Babcia only cooked twice a week, and the two retirees ate what Babcia made over and over again. And here I thought my days of cooking were over.

The two retirees, whom I was secretly calling the Shenanigan Sisters, bustled around the kitchen. Once again, I was told to sit at the table like a child. I hightailed it to the dining room table. No one had to tell me twice to sit and get served like a queen.

While I waited, I pulled out the cell phone that Malcolm had given me and stared at the screen. It was one thing to investigate Fiona's murder to keep ourselves out of jail, but it was another thing entirely to work for the local crime boss. What were we thinking, making a deal with the devil? When Aunt Coco slid a bowl in front of me, I put the phone back into the pocket of my hoodie.

General and Huntley hovered near the table, their eyes trained to the movement of our hands, as if waiting for one of us to drop food under the table. And the two of them were the first ones to get fed.

Once again, Aunt Coco opened a bottle of wine, but this time I was stopping at one glass. As we ate, we filled Babcia in on our conversations with Juan Perez and Malcolm Spencer.

"We're working with Malcolm now," Aunt Coco said, wiggling her eyebrows up and down.

Babcia perked up. "Mad Dog Spencer?"

"I told you he has the hots for me," Aunt Coco said.

"It's kind of hard to believe," Babcia said. "He hasn't looked at another woman since his wife died. And that date of yours at the waffle house sounded too much like something I've seen in a movie." She rubbed her chin and mumbled to herself, "Now what movie was it?"

I gave my aunt a sideways glance. So I wasn't the only one who felt that her date with the crime boss sounded like it belonged in Hollywood. "I thought he ran around with other women."

"That was before his wife died," Babcia said. "He must have seen the error in his ways."

I blinked. How did Babcia hear my comment? I sat on the side of her bad ear. Was her hearing selective? "Aunt Coco, how did you know Fiona wasn't his biological daughter?"

"Fiona wasn't adopted," Aunt Coco said.

"But you told Malcolm that Fiona wasn't his," I said.

"I heard that line in a movie, and I always wanted to say it out loud," Aunt Coco said.

Now I was confused. Malcolm had ignored the comment, much like he had ignored what my aunt had said the entire time. What crime boss did that? Was I starting to drink the Kool-Aid? Buying into the rumors around town because that was more exciting than a rich person with a security detail?

"Where do we stand on this murder investigation?" Babcia said.

Aunt Coco looked at me expectantly. "Aren't you writing down the clues?"

I looked at the Shenanigan Sisters and sighed inwardly. It felt like I was once again assigned a school project with people who only wanted to be the leader or presenter, but expected everyone else to do the work. And since there was no one else in this project, I was, by default, the worker bee. Oh, joy.

I went into the living room and grabbed the little notebook from my purse. At the kitchen table, I pushed my glasses up my nose and read my notes. "Duncan is out. He didn't have enough time to commit the crime. Juan is out. Malcolm and his goons are his alibis."

Babcia looked at Aunt Coco. "You didn't do it, did you? Tell us the truth. We wouldn't tell anyone else."

"No," Aunt Coco said. "I didn't kill Fiona."

"Then why are you on bail? Everly usually doesn't make mistakes," Babcia said.

This was the first time I heard Babcia speak well of the police. Maybe there was some truth to Evil Bun being a good cop.

Aunt Coco shifted in her seat.

I narrowed my eyes at my aunt. She was up to something.

As if reading my thoughts, Aunt Coco hurriedly said, "We need to focus on Juan. He's having an affair. We need to know his girlfriend's identity."

I gave my aunt a deadpan expression. What I didn't see, I didn't have to deal with. If she wanted to distract me, I would play along. Everyone was entitled to their harmless little secrets.

I reviewed everything again silently, my mind racing as I sought out any clues that I may have missed. My aunt was right. Even if Juan wasn't directly responsible for his wife's death, he probably had an idea of who did it.

"It's the girlfriend," Babcia said. "It's a crime of passion. She killed the wife so she could have the husband."

Aunt Coco clasped her hand in front of her chest and said in a dreamy voice, "I once had two boys fighting over me. I was the new girl at the high school, and Edward was obsessed with me. And then my friend Jacob started acting funny around me. Yada, yada later, and the two of them were at each other's throat. I pretended to have a seizure to stop the fighting." She rubbed her forehead. "I accidentally banged my head on the locker. What a racket that was."

Babcia and I shared a look. Here we were again.

Another one of Aunt Coco's crazy dating stories. Didn't my aunt meet my uncle when she was eighteen or nineteen? How much time did she have to date other people before they got together? As far as I knew, they had never broken up and were together since the dinosaur days.

"*Twilight*," Babcia mumbled under her breath.

I glanced at the window. Twilight? It was completely dark outside. I was beginning to feel like Alice at the tea party. Maybe the Shenanigan Sisters were raving mad, and I was the only sane one around here. "What?"

"Edward and Jacob are characters in *Twilight*, the books and the movies," Babcia mumbled under her breath.

Tickle me pink. Was my aunt for real? But this made a lot more sense. My aunt had always been a bibliophile. But I wasn't going to burst the bubble of her fictional world. "If we find the girlfriend, we find the killer."

"Personally, I wouldn't know why anyone would kill to have Juan Perez," Babcia said. "He's not even good looking."

"The heart wants what the heart wants," Aunt Coco said with a hand to her forehead. "If you look for an explanation for every relationship, then you haven't been madly in love before."

Babcia rubbed her chin. "I don't know about that. It's one thing to have a fling, but it's entirely another thing to be in a relationship. If a man wants to court me, he better come with a retirement fund because I'm not sharing mine. And I am too old to be a nurse maid." She wagged a finger at Coco. "And don't you get taken in by someone's sweet words."

I caught Babcia's eyes again and nodded. We were both secretly afraid that Aunt Coco would get bamboozled by a conman who would be after her money. But now that she had invested most of it at the tea shop, maybe she was a less appealing mark.

"Back to the investigation," I said. "We should do surveillance on Juan."

I told the Shenanigan Sisters about the straw dolls I'd seen in the backroom of Mary's costume shop.

"I thought the katana was a decoration." Aunt Coco's gaze swiveled to Babcia. "Did you know about the sword fighting?"

Babcia shook her head. "I never once suspected her. I knew about the broken engagement, but that was a long time ago. Mary has dated men since, though she has never come close to wedding bells with any one of them."

"Why is she in the Survivors Club?" I asked.

Babcia shrugged. "It's not like we ask each member for a death certificate. We didn't think someone would lie about something like this."

We were silent for a long moment.

"How do you think Mary fits into all this?" Aunt Coco said.

"Maybe she is the girlfriend," Babcia said.

"This is a long shot," I said. "Maybe she killed Fiona for stealing her fiancé."

"To wait over a decade before taking action, well, it doesn't feel like a crime of passion," Aunt Coco said.

"Who are we tailing tonight—Juan or Mary?" Babcia said.

I made a time-out sign with my hands. "We should watch a movie and go to bed early."

Aunt Coco and her friend exchanged a look. "We're doing surveillance on someone. You can either come with or you can stay home."

"I thought you two were tired," I said.

"I had my nap," Aunt Coco said.

"Me, too," Babcia said.

The Shenanigan Sisters stared at me—daring

me. If this wasn't a challenge, I didn't know what was. I couldn't let these two retirees go haring off on their own. One couldn't drive, and the other couldn't see to drive. They were accidents waiting to happen.

I made one last ditch effort to talk them out of it. "My truck is still parked in front of the tea shop, and Aunt Coco's car is in the body shop."

"You can drive my car," Babcia said.

I sighed and nodded reluctantly.

The Shenanigan Sisters beamed at each other.

"Who are we tailing again?" Babcia said.

"Juan," I said.

"Mary," Aunt Coco said.

"If we're wrong about Mary, Juan could meet up with his girlfriend while we are watching Mary," I said.

"We can always split up," Aunt Coco said.

I chewed on my lower lip. It made sense, but I didn't like the idea. In horror movies, the folks who went their separate ways got taken out one by one.

And how would we split up? I couldn't ask either of the two retirees to go out alone, which meant I would be alone. Even when I was younger, I wouldn't follow a man around in the dark.

As if hearing my thoughts, Aunt Coco said, "We can always ask Luke to help out."

I shook my head. "He has to get up at the crack of dawn to pick up Josh from the Redding airport."

Babcia and Aunt Coco shared a knowing look. Apparently, the matchmaking tendencies of little old ladies never went away. This was not my future. I would never play the matchmaker.

Aunt Coco set down her wine glass. "We can take care of this ourselves."

"So, who are we watching?" Babcia asked again.

"Juan," Aunt Coco said.

I pushed my glasses up my nose and reluctantly nodded.

Babcia gave my aunt a sly smile. "Are you thinking what I'm thinking?"

Aunt Coco wiggled her eyebrows. "Gabriel's footlocker."

The two women whooped and high-fived each other.

The dumpling soup turned in my stomach. "We're only getting the night vision goggles, right?"

The two women blinked at me. Finally Aunt Coco said, "Why don't you go take care of the dogs while we get ready for the late night surveillance."

I sighed inwardly. The Shenanigan Sisters wanted me out of their hair while they picked their weapons of mass destruction for tonight's surveillance. There was no harm in the retirees having a little fun with what could be an uneventful stakeout. But I didn't like them putting me in the parent role, like they had to sneak behind my back to get to their toys. When did I become their keeper? When did I become so boring?

## 21

## M.I.A

The Shenanigan Sisters went next door to look through Uncle Gabriel's footlocker while I cleaned up the dishes. Unlike Aunt Coco, Babcia didn't have a cleaning person come in, nor did she have any detergent for her dishwasher. It was a long time since I had to hand wash the dishes and pots, but this gave me the motivation to bird-dog my aunt's kitchen remodel.

First, this murder business. Second, the tea shop. And third, the kitchen remodel. It was just a checklist. As long as everyone stayed out of jail and no one got hurt, I could manage a checklist.

As I took the dogs around the block again, I was ready to turn in for the night. General didn't need to do any doggy business, but he happily trotted along with Huntley, and the two of them took turns peeing at other people's mailboxes. This was the kind of neighborhood where everyone had a unique mailbox on a post or column in front of the house instead of a communal mailbox area like in a planned subdivision.

A cell phone rang, and I jumped at the lyrics of "Macho Man." I pulled the vibrating device out of my hoodie pocket and tapped on the screen to get rid of the irksome noise. One of Malcolm's goons must have picked the ring tone. I made a mental note to change the ringtone to a children's song like "Baby Shark."

"Cedar?" my brother's voice came through the phone.

"Josh? How did you get this number?" I asked.

"Aunt Coco said you got a new cell phone."

"Did she tell you how I got it?"

"No."

For once, I had to give Aunt Coco credit for not spilling the beans. She had a habit of word vomiting when she spoke to us—mixing in gossip and secrets like they were the same thing.

"It's a loaner," I said. "I'm using it until I get this cell phone business sorted out. My old plan doesn't have reception here."

"I was able to get on a flight for tonight," Josh said. "I should be back in town by midnight. How about we have breakfast tomorrow morning?"

"Do you need me to pick you up from the airport?"

"Luke is coming to get me," Josh said. "How was your homecoming?"

"Did Aunt Coco tell you that her hip isn't broken?" I said dryly.

Josh chuckled. "Yeah, sorry about that. I misjudged the situation. At least you get to spend this weekend with us before you head home."

I grimaced. "I thought I'd be here for a few weeks. And when I asked for the time off, I got fired. And the landlord wanted the apartment back, so I turned in the key."

Josh was silent for a long moment. "It's only been a few days since we last talked. I can't believe so much has happened."

My brother seemed genuinely surprised, which meant he probably didn't know about Fiona's death or my aunt's involvement. There was no point in worrying him about it now. He would find out by tomorrow morning. "I have an appointment in the morning. Why don't we catch up at dinner?"

I didn't want to be the sacrificial lamb. When my

brother found out about the situation, he would blow a gasket. And he would come looking for our aunt, and I wasn't going to be anywhere near the vicinity. When titans collide, innocent bystanders like me could get hurt.

We made plans, and I hung up. I let myself into Babcia's kitchen and unleashed the dogs. General could spend the evening with his friend Huntley while we were at the stakeout.

The Shenanigan Sisters returned with a backpack on each of them, and we piled into Babcia's car. They gave me Juan's address, and I punched it into the GPS on the loaner phone. The dumpling soup churned in my stomach. Maybe I could still get my uneventful night sitting in the car.

I PARKED in front of Juan's house under the shadow of an oak tree. The single streetlight for the neighborhood was a block away. Unless Juan knew to look for us, it would be difficult for him to detect us.

I unbuckled my seatbelt and leaned back in the seat. It was going to be a long night.

Aunt Coco pulled out the night vision goggles,

binoculars, a thermal camera from the backpack and set them on the dashboard.

"What do you want to drink?" Babcia said. "I have Mountain Dew and Arizona iced tea."

"We need to stay hydrated," I said. If the Shenanigan Sisters kept drinking, maybe we could call it quits within an hour. One of them was bound to need a restroom.

"Tea, please," Aunt Coco said.

"Same. Thank you." I set the can on the dashboard with no intention of opening it.

"Want some chips?" Babcia said.

Aunt Coco nodded eagerly. "Yes, please."

As Babcia reached into the bag of chips, she knocked over her can of iced tea, spilling the liquid all over the backseat.

"Great," Babcia said.

I sighed and grabbed a handful of napkins from the glove compartment, passing them to Babcia. Luckily, this was her car and not mine.

Babcia mopped up the spill.

I turned my attention back to the house. It was a small, two-story building with a white fence enclosing the front yard. There were no lights on inside, and the street was quiet. Juan and his son were probably in bed.

I watched for any signs of movement, but the only thing that caught my eye was a stray cat darting across the street. I yawned. This was going to be a long night.

Babcia pulled out a bag of chocolate-covered espresso beans and offered some to Aunt Coco. "This should wake us up."

Aunt Coco yawned. "I haven't pulled an all-nighter since the boys were babies."

As the Shenanigan Sisters chewed on the beans, they traded stories from their youth. Their words became a steady hum. It was getting late, and my eyelids started to droop.

Suddenly, bright beams of light flooded the street, and I jolted in my seat. A police car with lights flashing and sirens blaring drove by, and I ducked down in the car, praying the Shenanigan Sisters had done the same. We remained still until the sound of the sirens faded away into nothing.

Once the coast was clear, I sat back up, fully awake again. That was close. Aunt Coco let out a huge sigh of relief and we all continued to watch the house. As minutes passed, my eyes began to droop again.

I woke to the peal of "Macho Man." Keeping my

eyes closed, I reached for the loaner cell phone. "Hello?" I mumbled.

"Cedar," said a familiar voice. "Josh is missing."

I sat up in my seat and rubbed my eyes. Where did Aunt Coco and Babcia go? I glanced at the dashboard. Midnight. The witching hour. And the time my brother was supposed to be back in town.

"Cedar, are you listening to me?" said the man on the phone.

"Who's this?" I said.

"It's Luke Kai. I'm at the airport, and I can't find your brother. His flight came in two hours ago, and the airline has confirmed that your brother was on the plane."

I eyed the dark street, looking for movement. A dog barked in the distance. Where were the Shenanigan Sisters? I should have turned on the car alarm. How could they sneak out without telling me? "Did you call his cell phone?"

My brother was a middle-aged, overweight man and smart enough to avoid dark alleys. He wasn't flashy enough to be a good mark for a ransom. However, I could see him helping a little old lady or a mother with young children somewhere at the airport.

"If I could reach your brother, do you think I would call you?" Luke snapped.

"Maybe his phone is out of power, and he needed to use the restroom," I said.

"Cedar, this is your brother we're talking about," Luke said.

I nodded even though Luke couldn't see me. Josh loved his little gadgets so much that he always carried around an extra power bank. "You're right. Something feels off about this. Did you talk to security?"

My brother wasn't the type to disappear without a word when he knew his friend made the long drive to the airport. Even if he was helping a little old lady, he would have called and left a message.

"Yes," Luke said. "But they won't let me review the video feeds without a missing person's report. And I can't file a missing person's report until tomorrow."

"I'm a little distracted right now. I had Aunt Coco and Babcia with me, and now they're both gone." My voice became shriller than normal.

Oh no. Oh no. They were all gone. My aunt. My brother. My breaths became quick and shallow, and I couldn't get enough air.

"Hey! Snap out of it." Luke's disgusted tone was enough to stop my spiraling thoughts.

I stiffened my spine. His words were like a slap in the face, and they snapped me back into focus. I took a deep breath. "Do you want me to drive to Redding to help you look? I need to get Aunt Coco and Babcia home first."

"Did you say they are missing, too?"

I explained that we were watching Juan's house. "I must have fallen asleep. Your call woke me up."

Luke swore. "I must've owed the Woods family in a previous life. First, your brother, and now, you and your aunt."

I bristled at his tone, feeling like a chastised child. I took another deep breath. This was not the time and place for an argument. I would be the bigger person.

"You didn't answer my question," I said. "Do you need me to come down to the airport?"

"No, I can take care of things at this end. It's a two-hour drive. Just get home safely and wait to see if Josh calls. Text me when you're home."

I promised to text him and hung up. I stared at the cell phone for half of a heartbeat. Even without the added stress of my missing brother, the conversation sounded a little too domesticated.

I slipped the loaner phone into my pocket and opened the door of the car. I saw Aunt Coco rounding the corner with the night vision goggles and peering into the windows at Juan's house. Babcia was next to her, eyes glued to the display of the thermal camera. If they were younger, the sight would have been disturbing. As it was, they looked like little old ladies with too much time on their hands.

The surveillance was a bust, and I was ready to call it a night. With my brother missing, I'd rather wait by the phone in the comfort of home.

A dark minivan with the headlights turned off glided up next to me underneath the shadow of the old tree. I almost jumped out of my skin. It must be an electric vehicle because I didn't hear any engine noise. I took a step out, and bumped into Babcia's car, banging my elbow. The side door slid open, and the faint dome light illuminated the floorboard and Josh's still body.

With my heart in my throat, I took a step closer, hands reaching out. My brother's hands and feet were bound, and his mouth was duct taped shut. Was my brother still breathing? There were visible signs of blood, but there was a metallic tang in the air. I checked for a pulse in his neck and breathed a sigh of relief. The pulse was faint but present. Josh was unconscious, but still alive.

I needed to call for an ambulance. As I straightened, I realized I was in a precarious situation. I glanced at the empty driver seat. Where was the minivan driver? How did this person know about my connection to Josh? Someone had targeted my brother and even knew his flight information. My brother must know the identity of this person. Was it Fiona's murderer?

From the corner of my eye, I saw movement. My head jerked back by instinct, and something hard cracked on the side of my head. If I hadn't moved, the heavy object would have smashed my face. I collapsed on top of my brother, disoriented. Blood streamed down my face, and my glasses hung lopsided from one ear. My eyes struggled to stay open. If I passed out now, I couldn't save my brother.

A black silhouette loomed over me and shoved my now useless legs into the minivan. With a ball cap pulled low and the hair in a ponytail, I couldn't make out the person's face, but I could tell my attacker was a woman. Juan's girlfriend? It had to be Mary Madden.

"Mary, stop," I rasped. My tongue felt thick in my

mouth. I wasn't even sure if the words came out or if I only made moaning sounds.

The woman wound duct tape around my hands and got back into the driver's seat. The air was filled with the coppery scent of blood and the musty odor of the van. She dropped the heavy object on the middle console.

Then I felt movement, and the minivan was no longer underneath the tree. The door slid closed, shutting out the sound of Aunt Coco's panicked voice calling my name. The object rolled back and dropped onto the floorboard with a crack. As the darkness closed in, I wondered if this was the last time I would hear my aunt's lovely voice.

## 22

## SMOKE SCREEN

When I came to, the minivan was no longer moving. Outside, it was pitch black. I squinted at the illumination from the van's headlight beams. Without my glasses, the world was a blur. I could make out the shapes of thick tree trunks but couldn't tell the species of the trees. The shadow of their branches stretched far into the night sky like gnarled hands. We were probably outside of town, on federal land.

Were we closer to the recreational area where Mary could drown us in the lake? But would she risk someone finding our bodies quickly? Or did she take one of the isolated mountain paths, which was dangerous to navigate in the dark? Once at the top, she could roll us off a cliff and our bodies wouldn't be discovered for months.

The driver's seat was empty. Where did Mary go? I couldn't tell if the engine was running, but I assumed it was because all the dashboard lights were still on. The electric minivan didn't have an ignition key slot, but one of those fancy pushbutton starters. I didn't see the key anywhere on the console. If I hopped onto the driver's seat, would I be able to get far without the key? Or would the engine shut down after a few feet?

I wiggled my hands and feet, trying to get rid of the pins-and-needles feeling. I gingerly touched the area around my temple, cringing as my fingers met a sticky substance. A quick inspection revealed that the wound was no longer bleeding.

I leaned over Josh, bringing his pale face into focus. His eyes were closed, and he was breathing shallowly, but he seemed alive and mostly unharmed—a far cry from what I'd expected when I first saw him on the floorboard of the van. With trembling hands, I shook my brother gently.

"Josh, wake up," I whispered.

My brother remained motionless, as if in a deep sleep.

"Wake up," I whispered again, my voice cracking.

Josh didn't move a muscle. My brother needed medical attention. I blinked back the tears in the back of my eyes. If I started crying now, I would be useless to us.

I considered my options. Running into the woods would give me a higher chance of surviving the night. It wasn't the tourist season, but it was still warm enough for some folks to camp with an RV.

But what about Josh? I wasn't strong enough to carry or drag my brother. And abandoning him wasn't an option. I wiped my clammy hands on my sweatpants. I had no choice. I had to stay and fight.

The knot of fear in my chest tightened, threatening to paralyze me if I gave into it. My hands were still bound together by the duct tape. I started tearing at it with my teeth. I was so frantic that I bit my wrist several times by accident. After a few moments of struggle, the duct tape finally came undone from my wrists.

I nervously glanced around the pitch-black minivan, but couldn't make out anything that I could use as a weapon. Without my glasses, and in the dark, I needed to rely on my ears and sense of touch.

I patted around the floorboard, looking for the heavy object Mary had used as a club. Should I turn on the light and risk Mary seeing me? I had no idea what she was doing outside the minivan. My fingers brushed against something hard, and I felt the first ray of hope. I had found the heavy object. As I felt along its wooden length, I recognized the shape of a rolling pin.

As I clutched the weapon in my hands, I frowned. Mary didn't seem like the type to have a rolling pin. And then everything fell into place. Our kidnapper wasn't Mary Madden—it was Chrissy Lane.

The assistant baker wasn't "sick" with a stomach flu. She was pregnant. I hadn't recognized the signs because I couldn't get pregnant during my marriage. Now, in hindsight, all the clues made sense. Chrissy was having an affair with Fiona's husband and got herself with a bun in the oven.

However, Juan couldn't just walk away from his marriage because of his father-in-law. So Chrissy took matters into her own hands and got rid of her romantic rival.

And Luke and I had probably interrupted Chrissy going through Fiona's purse in the walk-in pantry. The irony was that Fiona was planning to divorce her husband. If Chrissy had waited, she would have gotten what she wanted.

I did a quick assessment of our situation. I still

had the loaner cell phone, but I had no idea where we were. I probably had one chance to make a phone call or send a text message, and I needed to make sure the rescue squad knew where to find us. Somewhere on federal land was a big spot to cover.

I needed to take a quick look around outside the minivan to get my bearings. But what could I see without my glasses? I patted around the floorboards again, praying I would find them. After several frantic seconds, I came to the conclusion I wasn't going to find them.

Grimacing, I tucked the bloody rolling pin into the inner pocket of my parka. My stomach heaved at the thought of the dried blood, but I didn't have time to wipe it off. If caught, I had to keep Chrissy talking. Any minute we stayed alive was another minute for rescue to get here.

Then the headlights turned off, along with the dashboard lights. I almost jumped out of my skin. The electric vehicle probably turned off its engine or went into power saving mode. It was, after all, one big smart device with an electronic brain that believed it was smarter than the end user.

I heard Chrissy curse. She was somewhere near the trunk of the minivan. This was my sign to get moving. Maybe I could sneak up on her and whack her with the rolling pin like she did to me.

I pressed the button on the minivan door, and it glided open silently. A symphony of sounds hit me —chirping crickets, croaking frogs, and the distant hoot of an owl. Water lapped against the shoreline. We were at Trinity Lake, so close that I could make out the faint glimmer of moonlight reflecting off its waters. The air was thick with the musk of wet dirt and pine needles.

I pulled out the loaner cell phone and fired off a quick text message to my aunt.

CHRISSY IS THE KILLER AND KIDNAPPER. TRINITY LAKE.

I hit the send button. It took about forty minutes to drive around the lake. Even if our luck held out, it would still take some time before the rescue squad could get here.

Taking one last deep breath, I stepped out of the van, and my feet sunk up to my ankles in the mud. This explained why the minivan wasn't moving. Chrissy must have tried to get close to the edge of the lake and gotten the tires stuck in the mud. Josh and I were too heavy to drag to the water, and she couldn't abandon the vehicle. But neither could she let us live to point the finger at her. If this were a sitcom, the situation would be comedic. As it was, it made Chrissy dangerous like a cornered momma bear.

The chill night air hit me like a wave and I shivered involuntarily, wishing that I could see something other than darkness ahead of me. The gentle rustling of leaves above me as an occasional breeze brushed against them lightly was more eerie than comforting.

The driver's door opened, and I ducked around the back of the van. Maybe I could get Chrissy to confess her crime. Didn't all the bad guys like to talk in the movies about how smart they were? As I tapped on the recorder app, a shadow loomed over me and grabbed the cell phone from my hands. I stumbled back and bumped my elbow into the minivan, my hand going numb for a split second as pain raced down my arm.

"Why are you doing this, Chrissy?" I said. "Is it worth it to commit murder for Juan?"

The shadows stiffened, and she took off her ball cap. The moonlight broke from the clouds overhead, and my kidnapper's face was a blur in front of me. In one hand, she clutched the loaner cell phone, and in her other hand, she held onto what I assumed was a shovel based on the shape of the object. The tool she had used to clear the mud away from the tires was now her weapon against me. "Can you see me?"

I held up my hand. "I can't even see my hand. Did you take my glasses?" While my vision was limited, my hearing had sharpened to compensate for it. "But I figured it was either you or Mary Madden. And your voice confirmed your identity."

Chrissy snorted like she was amused. Maybe she thought I wasn't much of a threat.

"Did you kill Fiona to have Juan to yourself?" I asked.

"I didn't kill Fiona for Juan," Chrissy said. "I killed her to get back at Malcolm Spencer."

I blinked in surprise, thoroughly confused. "You're having an affair with Malcolm? He's old enough to be your grandfather."

Chrissy laughed bitterly. "No, you dumb bimbo."

I took a deep breath. Trading insults wouldn't help the situation. I needed to keep Chrissy talking to buy us more time. Maybe I could appeal to her vanity. Didn't most criminals like to believe they were smarter than everyone else? "Then explain it to me. Why did you kill Fiona? And how did you get away with it?"

"Malcolm ruined my family." Chrissy stepped closer, the shovel shaking in her hands. "My father killed himself when our family business went bankrupt, and my mother died of a broken heart soon after. I grew up with foster families. Moving every few months. Never having a family."

I took a step back. Maybe I could de-escalate the situation if we appeared to have common ground. "I understand. I was an orphan, too. Why didn't you kill Malcolm? Isn't he the person who deserves to be punished?"

"I can't get to him. I pretended to be friends with that psycho daughter of his, hoping to get a chance to sit across from Malcolm at the dinner table where I could slip him something. I never got the opportunity, so Fiona was my next best option. At least I know this will hurt."

"Then how does Juan factor into this? Why did you have an affair with him?"

Chrissy snickered. "I wouldn't touch that man with a ten-foot pole. Juan is having an affair with Mary Madden and paying me hush money."

My eyes widened. Shut the door. Juan had asked for more time that day in the office because she was blackmailing him. What else did I get wrong? "Are you pregnant? Who's the father?"

"Maybe it's Luke Kai," Chrissy said.

I didn't like the self-satisfied tone in her voice. While I couldn't make out the expression on her face, I was sure she was smiling. Why did she think I would care who Luke was sleeping with? Was it because she saw the two of us together investigating the murder?

I strained my ears, listening for the rescue squad. How much more time did I need to make "small talk" with a murderer? "How did you kidnap my brother? How did you know the details of his flight information?"

"There are truly no secrets in this town. I was in the kitchen talking to Hazel when Luke came by for sandwiches. While she was making them, he talked about picking up Josh at the airport later that evening. I heard all the details from inside the kitchen."

Holy macaroni. Luke the blabbermouth struck again. The man was a menace. How in the world did I find him attractive? He was worse than a gossip girl from high school.

The "Macho Man" ringtone filled the air. Chrissy jumped and dropped the loaner cell phone. I whipped the rolling pin out of my parka and knocked the shovel out of her hands. The cell phone continued to vibrate and ring in the mud. Once the call went to voicemail, the caller called back again, and "Macho Man" filled the air again. It almost seemed as if someone was using the cell phone to locate us.

I heard a faint twang like something was launched from a slingshot. A smoking canister landed at Chrissy's feet.

*Plunk! Plunk!*

Smoke grenades rained down all around us. I registered Chrissy's surprised face for a split second and then the gray smoke filled the air between us. I couldn't see more than the hand in front of my face. Chrissy had lost her previous advantage—now both of us were blind.

I sidestepped. Staying put was akin to being a sitting duck. The faint pitter patter of running feet meant the rescue squad was here.

Something hurled itself at my previous location. I struck at my feet, and Chrissy crashed onto the ground next to me. Before I could react, she grabbed my ankle and yanked, dragging me down.

I kicked out, but I couldn't dislodge Chrissy's grip. My blood pounded in my ears. Rescue was mere minutes away. I wasn't giving up at the eleventh hour.

An animal barked, and the crackle of walkie-talkies filled the air. Movement from the corner of my eye caught my attention. General charged out of the smoke and landed on Chrissy's back. His warning growl turned Chrissy into a statue, and her hand released my ankle.

I scuttled back on my butt. As the adrenaline left my body, I felt weak all over. I didn't have any more fight in me.

The smoke cleared, Aunt Coco and Babcia came out of the woods, holding homemade slings for launching the smoke grenades.

"Freeze in the name of the law," Aunt Coco yelled.

"We got weapons, and we're not afraid to use them," Babcia said.

The Shenanigan Sisters waved the slings around like they were nunchucks. If I wasn't still trying to catch my breath, I might have burst out laughing.

Officers came out of the woods, guns drawn and pointing their weapons at us.

Chief Blunt yelled, "Drop your weapon! Drop your weapon!"

Chrissy held her hands up in the air. "Officers, Cedar Woods kidnapped me. She wants to kill me."

"Drop your weapon," Chief Blunt yelled again.

I glanced around, confused. And then it hit me that I was still holding the bloody rolling pin.

"Cedar, drop it!" Aunt Coco yelled. General got off of Chrissy and joined my aunt.

I dropped the wooden object and held up both hands. "I have proof that Chrissy is the kidnapper and Fiona's killer. The cell phone recorded our conversation."

Chrissy's eyes widened, and she made a desperate dive for the loaner cell phone. Probably to destroy the evidence.

Chief Blunt fired off a shot in the air, and Chrissy flinched, dropping the cell phone in fright. Two officers closed in on Chrissy quickly, restraining and handcuffing her. Then one of them collected the cell phone as evidence.

"I can't believe you made me waste a bullet," Chief Blunt said, scowling at me. "Couldn't you have waited until Chrissy was in handcuffs before mentioning the cell phone?"

I gave Evil Bun a sheepish look. "Sorry. I didn't know who you would believe, and I didn't want to be shot by accident."

Chief Blunt walked over to me with hands on her hips. "Weird Wood, I already told you that you're not bullet worthy."

I didn't know what to make of the comment, but now wasn't the time to noodle on it. "Josh is in the minivan, and he needs medical attention."

Chief Blunt spoke into the walkie talkie clipped to her shoulder and jogged over to the van.

Aunt Coco hurled herself into my arms. "Cedar, are you okay? I'm sorry we weren't able to get here sooner. Malcolm helped us track the GPS signal from the cell phone."

I nodded. My throat was too tight to speak. I watched over the top of my aunt's head as a disheveled Chrissy was loaded into a police cruiser, handcuffs binding her hands. My gaze lingered on her.

For a moment, I was thankful I never knew my biological family. What I didn't know, I didn't miss. I wasn't sure I could bear the pain of losing them any better than Chrissy.

## 23

-----

# TEA TIME

The next morning, I woke to doggie breath in my face and my body aching like I had run a marathon. I pushed General away and reached for my glasses. My hand patted around the side table for several seconds before my brain fired up. My glasses were still M.I.A.

I stumbled out of bed and into the hallway bathroom to put in my contacts. A few minutes later I was ready to face the day. As I made my way downstairs, the doorbell rang. I stepped into the living room just as Aunt Coco opened the door for Chief Blunt in the foyer. I padded over to the entryway to eavesdrop. I didn't realize I was such a snoop until I started investigating Fiona's murder.

As much as I appreciated Evil Bun's timely

rescue last night, making friendly small talk with my arch-nemesis wasn't how I wanted to start my day.

Aunt Coco and Chief Blunt exchanged pleasantries, and my aunt invited the police chief to stay for breakfast.

Chief Blunt looked as if she hadn't slept in a week, but she smiled for once. I bet the rumor mill around town was working overtime. And Chief Blunt might have secured her position for the rest of her career.

"No, thanks, Coco," Chief Blunt said. "I want to thank you for luring out the killer."

I blinked. What was Evil Bun talking about? Chrissy Lane had come after me, not my aunt. Not that I needed the police chief's acknowledgment of my role in capturing Fiona's killer. I didn't need her approval.

Aunt Coco waved away Chief Blunt's words. "Just doing my part as a Good Samaritan."

"I couldn't believe your plan worked," Chief Blunt said.

Aunt Coco beamed. "I dated a police chief once—"

"I can't believe you didn't tell your niece," Chief Blunt cut in, probably hoping she wouldn't have to hear one of my aunt's infamous dating stories.

"Tell me what?" I said, stepping into the foyer.

Both Aunt Coco and Chief Blunt glanced in my direction, startled. My aunt looked guilty, and the police chief looked amused.

Aunt Coco averted her gaze. "I volunteered for Everly to charge me for killing Fiona."

My jaw dropped. Shut the door. I started sleep-walking again because my aunt wanted to role-play. "Aunt Coco, I was really worried about you going to jail."

Aunt Coco placed her hands together as if in prayer. "I'm sorry, Cedar Bear, but Everly wanted Chrissy to feel like she got away with murder. It was the only way to lure her into making a mistake."

I glanced at my arch nemesis. "You knew it was Chrissy Lane all along?"

"I couldn't verify her alibi," Chief Blunt said.

I frowned, trying to recall what the assistant baker had said. "Wasn't she at the drugstore picking up medication?"

"Yes, but there was half an hour unaccounted for," Chief Blunt said.

"Forensics were able to pinpoint the time of death so precisely?" I asked.

"The backdoor camera at one of the homes next to the back alley recorded the time someone entered and left the area," Chief Blunt said. "The video was too blurry to identify the person, so we had to resort to old fashioned trickery to get the killer to reveal herself."

I was impressed with Evil Bun's detective work, but I still didn't like her involving my elderly aunt. "But how did you know Chrissy would do something? What if she lay low until things blew over?"

Chief Blunt studied me for a long moment. "I was counting on you."

I blinked, not quite following Evil Bun's logic. "Excuse me?"

"Your aunt told me everything you had discovered during her interview at the police station."

I shot my aunt a look. So Luke wasn't the only blabbermouth I should be careful around. "But it wasn't much."

"It was enough for me to know you could piece things together. What wasn't said was equally important as what was said." Chief Blunt rubbed the scar on her chin with her thumb. "Remember how you stood up to me for picking on someone half my size when we were kids?"

I nodded reluctantly. "She was two grades younger than us. I didn't want to fight, but you gave me no choice."

"I was counting on you to keep digging and applying pressure against the other suspects after your aunt's arrest. And when you showed up with Fiona's purse, I knew I made the right choice."

"So you used me," I said, not bothering to hide my annoyance.

"I didn't have staff to help me with the murder investigation. My officers still had their regular duties, and they didn't have the instinct to question the suspects. I had to use what resources were available." Chief Blunt glanced at my aunt. "And Coco volunteered the both of you."

Aunt Coco beamed like I had won the spelling bee. "I told you my girl could do it."

"I need to confiscate your phone," Chief Blunt said. "It's evidence."

I nodded, expecting as much. I hoped Malcolm didn't expect me to reimburse him. It was the price for finding his daughter's killer. Maybe I could send Malcolm the bill for my new glasses.

Chief Blunt thanked the two of us again and left. I followed my aunt to the kitchen, still miffed at being kept in the dark. General padded after us, his tongue hanging out like he was enjoying a secret joke.

Aunt Coco poured the hot water into mugs for

tea. She handed me the little white bags from the bakery, and we sat in the patio chairs set on the back porch to eat our breakfast. I could get used to having a fresh pastry each morning, but I should join my aunt on her morning walk if I wanted to keep eating them.

General raced into the backyard and returned in a few minutes with Huntley. The two dogs sniffed at plants and came up to us. Aunt Coco gave General a long scratch behind his ears, patted Huntley, and shooed them away. The two dogs bounded away, eager to continue their game of chase.

As I munched on the butter croissant and the autumn sun warmed my skin, I was finally home. Here with my aunt and her dog—getting pampered by my family.

"I'm sorry for not telling you about my arrangement with Everly," Aunt Coco said.

I brushed the crumbs off my shirt. "Why did you think it was a good idea?"

Aunt Coco pointed at General. "It was his plan."

"You're blaming the dog?"

"I'm acknowledging his contribution."

I chuckled. "Do you believe General is Uncle Gabriel?"

Aunt Coco shrugged. "Does it matter? Is it harming anyone?"

I considered my aunt's questions for a long moment. "What about you? What if people think you're not quite right in the head?"

Aunt Coco shrugged again. "What is wrong with being a bit different than everyone else?"

"But this sets you apart from everyone else." My thoughts shifted to how I was called Weird Wood until my high school graduation. "They'll start rumors about you."

"They already call me Coconut, so I might as well give them something to talk about. At my age, I'm either crazy or eccentric. They should be thankful I still wear my bra in public."

"You are right," I said. "It doesn't matter if General is Uncle Gabriel's reincarnated spirit or a guardian angel. He's looking out for us, and that's good enough for me."

General and Huntley started barking at a squirrel up in a tree. The fluffy-tailed critter yelled back at the two dogs, which only made them bark more and made my aunt laugh.

Wiping away the happy tears from her eyes, Aunt Coco smiled at me. "General is such a comfort to me."

"What about Huntley?" I asked. "Is he someone we know?"

"He's just a dog."

"Hey, I've got to ask. The two of them seem to be good friends. I never imagined my three-star general uncle sniffing somebody's butt."

Aunt Coco gave me a deadpan look. "You might have to pour bleach in your ears if I tell you some of the things your uncle has done."

I threw an arm around my aunt's shoulders and hugged her. "Love you, Aunt Coco."

Aunt Coco patted my forearm. "Cedar Bear, I am so happy that you're finally home."

THREE WEEKS LATER, Main Street in Old Town was blocked off for the Fall Festival. The air was thick with the smells of popcorn and hot dogs, and laughter and music filled the air. Booths lined the street, some with homemade goods, others with crafts and trinkets. At one end, a stage was set up for local bands to play throughout the day.

The sun shone in the cloudless sky, and the town buzzed with energy. People were out and about, browsing the stalls and talking to friends, a few of them in costumes, along with their children. The shop windows were decorated with fall colors, and the Old Town Business Association had arranged pumpkins, haystacks, and scarecrows at several locations for photo ops.

Aunt Coco, Josh, and I were in our *Alice in Wonderland* costumes handing out postcards about the tea shop with a ten percent off discount. And General preened under the bunny ears, lapping up all the pats on the head from everyone. Even if we lost the costume contest, we still came out ahead for all the attention we generated for the tea shop.

I couldn't believe the Super Mario Brothers had completed their remodeling on time. The interior of the whimsical tea shop was decorated with vibrant colors, oversized mushrooms, and indoor plants to resemble a secret garden. It was a bit kooky, but it worked to set us apart from the Gold Rush era decor of the surrounding shops.

But instead of a traditional tearoom, my aunt sold traditional teas, Boba teas, and a small selection of Chinese dim sum and pastries—here in Mirror Falls! No wonder she wasn't afraid of competition. And she had hired all Fiona's staff—minus her killer —so we didn't have to do everything ourselves. The townsfolk were still hesitant about the menu and the chewy tapioca balls, but the tourists loved them. My concern was overrated.

When there was a break in the crowd, my brother, Josh, ambled over. Though he had put on the dormouse costume without protest, he had added a whip to the belt on his hip and a wide-brim Fedora. As much as I loved my brother, whip cracking was a weird hobby. He was one of the few people I knew who wanted to become Indiana Jones as a child and grew up to become a middle-aged version of his hero. Too bad it didn't give him enough street smarts to avoid getting a crack on the head.

I gestured at the bench on the boardwalk. "Let's take a break." I handed my brother the rest of the postcards. "I'll get us a snack from the kitchen."

Josh dropped onto the bench and took off his hat. "Sounds good."

Though my brother seemed to have gotten over his mild concussion, I was still concerned. This was his first outing, and I was afraid to tire him out. From the corner of my eye, I saw a flash of black and red flannel. I glanced over my shoulder to see Luke talking with someone and sneaking glances at my brother. Nice. I wasn't the only one keeping an eye on Josh.

I went into the kitchen and got two Boba milk teas—lychee oolong for my brother, black lavender cream for me—and a few pot stickers. I handed my brother the plastic cup and straw and set the bamboo plate between us. We munched in silence for several long minutes, people-watching.

"I can't believe everything all worked out." I gestured at the line forming outside the tea shop. "And this was beyond my wildest expectations."

Josh swallowed the bite in his mouth. "This is my speculation, but I think Aunt Coco did it for you."

I blinked, taken aback. "Me? What do you mean?"

"To keep you busy and lure you back in town. Even though Aunt Coco never said anything, I have a feeling she is lonely."

Josh's cell phone rang, and he pulled it out of his pocket. He tapped the screen, letting it go into voicemail. "Probably another scammer calling about my car warranty. Where were we?"

"Aunt Coco being lonely," I said. "But you're in town, and she has friends."

"I have work and my hobbies. Besides, you've always been her favorite. All of us boys know this."

I rolled my eyes. "Aren't we too old to be whining about favorites?"

"For you, maybe," Josh said, his eyes twinkling. "For me? Nope. I know I'm second-hand chopped liver."

I chuckled, knowing there were no hurt feelings involved with my brother. The enormity of what would happen hit me out of the blue, and the remaining humor disappeared. "I have never run a business before. What if I fail?"

"Then I guess I'll have to take you both in," Josh said, shrugging. "It's not like I would turn you or Aunt Coco out on the streets."

I cleared my throat. "Is Luke the father of Chrissy's baby?"

Josh's eyes widened in surprise. "The last few years have been hard on him—too many family members dying off. He doesn't have room on his plate for anyone else right now."

"He didn't seem to like me much. Do you know why?"

Josh opened his mouth but was interrupted by a ping on his cell phone. He listened to the voicemail message, frowning. He blinked several times and tapped on the screen again. "Listen to this." His voice came out hoarse with emotion.

"Joshua Woods? This is Bonnie Wong. You don't know me, but I found your daughter, Willow Joo, living in the streets of San Francisco. We are coming up to Mirror Falls in two days." There were some scuffling noises and a faint conversation. The person returned to the phone. "Willow is your daughter with Kim."

My brother's hand shook, and the cell phone dropped onto the boardwalk.

My eyes widened. Kim Joo was my brother's former fiancée—the one who got away. "When was the last time you and Kim..."

"When she broke off our engagement." Josh licked his lower lip. "Thirteen years ago."

Want to meet Bonnie Wong and Willow Woods?
Bag the Body
(Cedar Woods Mystery #2)

Or come meet Raina Sun and Bonnie Wong
Raining Men and Corpses
(Raina Sun Mystery #1)

## ACKNOWLEDGMENTS

A story is a dream that a writer brings to life on paper. But a book needs a team to nurture it into the enjoyable tale you've just read.

I want to thank my editors, Bev R. and Alicia S., for wrangling my words so they are coherent.

And then, there are my wonderful beta-readers—Della D., Debi P., Joyce S., Karyn S., Marion D., and one anonymous reader—thank you, ladies, for volunteering your time to catch sneaky typos, grammatical errors, and missing children (Malcolm Spencer needed more children for Duncan to be Fiona's nephew. Not sure how this one sneaked by.).

I wouldn't have been able to bring this story to life without all of you, wonderful ladies. Thank you!

—Anne R. Tan

# ALSO BY ANNE R. TAN

Thanks for reading *Arrest the Alibi*. I hope you enjoyed it!

## Did you like this book?

Please review my books at my website or your *favorite retailer*. As an indie author, reviews help other readers find my books. I appreciate all reviews, whether positive or negative.

## Want to know about new releases, sale pricing, and exclusive content?

Sign up for Anne R. Tan's Readers Club newsletter at http://annertan.com

Your information would not be sold or transferred. Thank you for trusting me with your email.

## Want more Cedar Woods?

*Bag the Body* (Cedar Woods #2) - coming Fall 2024

## Have you met Raina Sun?

*Raining Men and Corpses* (Raina Sun #1)

*Gusty Lovers and Cadavers* (Raina Sun #2)

*Breezy Friends and Bodies* (Raina Sun #3)

*Balmy Darlings and Death* (Raina Sun #4)

*Sunny Mates and Murders* (Raina Sun #5)

*Murky Passions and Scandals* (Raina Sun #6)

*Smoldering Flames and Secrets* (Raina Sun #7)

*Hazy Grooms and Homicides* (Raina Sun #8)

*Chilly Comforts and Disasters* (Raina Sun #9)

*Fair Cronies and Felonies* (Raina Sun #10)

*Airy Allies and Enemies* (Raina Sun #11)

**How about another series by Anne R. Tan?**

*Just Shoot Me Dead* (Lucy Fong #1)

*Just Lost and Found* (Lucy Fong #1.5)

*Just a Lucky Break-In* (Lucy Fong #2)

# ABOUT THE AUTHOR

Anne R. Tan, a *USA Today* bestselling author, writes the Raina Sun Mystery series, Lucy Fong Mystery series, and the Cedar Woods Mystery series. Her humorous mysteries feature Chinese-American sleuths and diverse characters because everyone deserves to be an armchair detective.

Sign up for her newsletter for new release announcement, sales, and exclusive content at https://annertan.com

A NOTE FROM ANNE:

My books are my legacy to my children. They will not grow up in the San Francisco Bay Area like I did. Without a cultural hub, our family would lose this part of our heritage in one generation. My children are visitors to Chinese culture, just like my readers. At its core, Chinese culture is about family and community. And my characters—Raina Sun, Lucy

Fong, Cedar Woods, and their dynamic family—embody these values in every chapter. Come experience the vibrant world I've created. I promise you'll enjoy reading my books as much as I've loved writing them.

~Anne

Made in United States
Troutdale, OR
08/13/2023

12033829R00190